he could barely form the words.

"Just go away. I'm really not in the mood."

"Claire-bear—"

"Don't. You lost the right to call me that a long time ago." Claire grabbed her purse. "I'm done here. If this silly competition is what this town wants in a mayor, I'm obviously not their choice."

Evan caught her arm as she turned to leave. "You're not a coward. Stop choosing to quit."

"I don't *choose* it."

"You're choosing it now, and you did it every time when you wouldn't let me explain about the past."

She yanked her arm away. "How dare you."

He blocked her retreat. "The Claire I knew and loved had the fire to match her hair. That Claire would never give up. I miss her."

She wanted to toss back an angry barb. Fuel the fight so she didn't have to admit the truth of his words.

"Do what makes you happy, Claire," he prompted. "What do you love?"

You.

Her stomach tightened. That couldn't be right. She didn't love Evan Daniels.

She couldn't…

Jessica Keller is a Starbucks drinker, avid reader and chocolate aficionado. Jessica holds degrees in communications and biblical studies. She is multipublished in both romance and young adult fiction and loves to interact with readers through social media. Jessica lives in the Chicagoland suburbs with her amazing husband, beautiful daughter and two annoyingly outgoing cats who happen to be named after superheroes. Find all her contact information at jessicakellerbooks.com.

The Single Mom's Second Chance

Jessica Keller

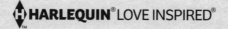

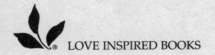 LOVE INSPIRED BOOKS

Recycling programs
for this product may
not exist in your area.

ISBN-13: 978-0-373-89936-4

The Single Mom's Second Chance

www.Harlequin.com

Printed in U.S.A.

Wait for the Lord;
be strong and take heart and wait for the Lord.
—*Psalms* 27:14

For the boy I fell in love with at eighteen
who became the man still holding my heart
all these years later.

Chapter One

Claire Atwood brushed snowflakes from her shoulder as she waited for her son to shut the back door of her car.

"Hurry up, Alex. This has to be turned in by four." Claire tucked the leather portfolio tighter under her arm. She didn't want the paperwork that would guarantee she'd be added to the ballot for the open mayoral position to tumble out.

She motioned for Alex to speed up and join her down the walkway leading to the town hall. A shiver worked its way through her, making her wish she'd tugged on her down jacket instead of the thinner peacoat when they were still back at home. Ice crystals formed lace patterns on the front windows of the building. *February frost.* That's what

Mom called it back when Claire was still a child, too many years ago.

She puffed out a breath and watched it spiral in the crisp air before vanishing.

Overall, Goose Harbor had enjoyed a rather mild winter this season—more slush than snowfall, really—which was part of the problem. From spring through fall the lake and the beautiful dunes brought people from miles away to explore their quaint little town, and they depended on the charm of winter to continue drawing tourists December through March for revenue. Overall, tourism was the most profitable trade in Goose Harbor. Fresh snow brought couples to the area for romantic horse-drawn sleigh rides, holiday celebrations and ice-skating, and also pulled people to come enjoy the multiple Christmas and New Year's events around town. One of the local bed-and-breakfasts held Charles Dickens's Christmas weekend getaways and people dressed up like old-time carolers for the tree lighting festival. But the warmth this year had kept the number of visitors slim.

Dismal, really.

Claire tightened her hold on her portfolio and turned toward town hall. She could do this. Help her hometown. Do something with her life that mattered beyond credentials and degrees and being the daughter of tycoon Sesser Atwood.

The building sat across the street from Lake Michigan in the downtown section. Up the path and to the right of town hall stood the charming brick chamber of commerce building and the equally enchanting library. After those buildings there were storefronts and restaurants—everything Goose Harbor was known for. However, town hall was a long, white unassuming structure, as well as one of the oldest buildings in town. In spring, green flower boxes lined the many windows, but for now it was bare, besides the American flag flapping near the white double doors that led inside. Light flurries swirled around the dormer windows at the very top of the building.

Alex rammed his hands deep into the pockets of his coat and trudged up the path. His thick, dark hair hung in front of his eyes. "Why did I have to come?"

Because you're my son. I want you with me.

Five minutes to four wasn't the time for a long emotional conversation. Especially not when the sky had finally decided to open up and dump some lake effect snow onto their corner of Michigan.

Claire sucked in a cold burst of air, sending a shock down into her lungs that rattled her. "Please, just behave. Okay?"

The seven-year-old stumbled beside her. "I don't want to be here."

Here as in in front of town hall? Or did he mean in America, with her, as her adopted son? No, she didn't want to know the answer to that question. Sometimes the unknown was far kinder than discovering the truth.

Still, she should acknowledge what Alex said. The family therapist they'd been meeting with since she'd brought Alex home had explained to Claire how important it was for her son to feel heard.

She stopped walking. "Where else would you rather be?"

He dragged the toe of his shoe through the fresh powder on the ground. "You could have left me at home with your parents."

Your parents.

When she'd flown to Russia eight months ago and adopted Alexei—who started going by Alex once he began school last fall—Claire had thought becoming a mother would solve all her problems. She'd have someone to love who would love her back. Someone who would want her. Need her.

As it turned out, Alex didn't want her. She might as well get it stitched onto a pillow so she'd never forget: You Are Not Wanted or You Will Always Be Alone. Something snazzy like that to freshen up the artfully decorated apartment area of her parents' home she called her own.

Claire didn't know what to do with his attitude or how to help Alex anymore. She was failing. Like usual. Only now, her inability was affecting more than just her.

She squatted, trying to avoid getting her pants wet, and placed a hand on his shoulder. "They're your grandparents."

He skewed his face. "Not really."

"Yes, really."

"If you say, then it is so." The missionaries who worked alongside the orphanage Alex had been adopted from started teaching him English soon after his fifth birthday. So thankfully, when Claire met him in Russia last year, they'd been able to communicate. He still struggled with proper phrasing, but most of the time he did really well with his second language.

The double doors to town hall parted with a click and then a whoosh of air.

Alex jerked away from Claire and side-stepped her, bolting forward. "Evan!"

"Hey there, bud. Let me get the door for you guys." The smooth, rich voice of Evan

Daniels jolted through Claire. Causing her heart to hammer as if she'd downed a triple shot of espresso.

Then everything stalled. How did Evan know her son?

A chill traveled up Claire's neck. She'd successfully been living back in Goose Harbor for more than a year without having to face Evan Daniels. She'd gone out of her way to avoid all contact with him. The man and the past they shared had been her one hesitation about returning home after she broke off her engagement to Auden Pierce back in New York.

Except now here he was in the flesh, only a few feet away, a tentative grin showing off the gorgeous smile he'd always possessed. Evan had definitely won the DNA jackpot—square jaw, a body shaped by long hours doing carpentry and dark hair that he still styled to look slightly mussed. And his eyes? Crisp, hard-to-look-away-from greens. It was the shade of green that infused life into the air, the type that poked through the last of the snow after a harsh winter and dotted the bare limbs of the trees, hinting at the hope of spring.

Hope.

A word that hardly fit the man.

He would have enjoyed a successful career

modeling—probably still could if he wanted to. If Evan continued to possess half the charm he'd flashed her way in high school, the man could become the next reality show host wearing a three-piece suit as he interviewed and consoled the latest person kicked out of whatever competition. Or he could become some heartthrob on the fix-it channel—that would be right up his alley. If he'd pursued a career like that, he would no longer be living in Goose Harbor and that would have made Claire much happier. Instead of how he was right now, standing there in a peacoat, a blue-and-gray-plaid scarf around his neck, looking so appealing.

"Claire," he whispered as he tipped his head.

Her name didn't belong on his lips like that. Not said so sweetly, gently.

Head down, she brushed past him. "We haven't talked in twelve years. Let's not start now." She barreled into the town hall's lobby. The sweet, almost watermelon smell of his hair pomade followed her. He must still use the same brand he had in high school. So like Evan. Steady, constant, loyal to a brand.

Just not to Claire.

Emotion balled in her throat for a moment, but she shoved it away.

Don't be ridiculous.

"Come on, Alex," she called without looking back. An icy wind hit her, making long red strands of her hair dance in front of her face. Letting her know Evan still held the door.

Alex brought her up short with a hand on her arm. "Can't I stay with Mr. Evan?"

She latched on to her son's wrist and tugged him toward the wide front desk in the lobby, where Mrs. Clarkson, an eccentric old lady known around town for wearing clothes she'd knit out of socks or upholstery material, folded a pamphlet detailing frequently asked questions about utility bills.

Mrs. Clarkson rested her hands on top of the pamphlet and smiled over at them as if completing one piece out of the four-inch stack beside her was a huge accomplishment that they should acknowledge with a round of applause. Yellow edged her teeth from years of guzzling coffee.

Claire made a mental note to call her dentist and set up a whitening appointment. Maybe even halve her personal coffee consumption, as well. *Ha. Not likely.* The three or four cups she was currently downing were barely keeping her running as it was.

Claire craned her head toward Alex and

spoke in a low voice. "How do you even know that man?"

"Mr. Evan?" He brushed his shaggy hair from his eyes. "He helps in Sunday school."

"I've never seen him when I dropped you off. Don't the Holcombs—Toby and Jenna, your friend Kasey's parents—don't they run your class?"

"Well, yeah. But Mr. Evan helps, too. He's some kind of big deal in children's ministry." Alex angled his head. "He's late to my class and has to go early because he directs traffic and greets."

Of course. She knew about those things and should have guessed about his additional involvement. Since returning to Goose Harbor Claire had noticed that Evan had his hands in just about every part of town—helping on several committees, building the sets for the local play troupe and volunteering at most of the seasonal events.

Once Evan became a greeter at church Claire had opted for entering through the side door. Not that she thought she could avoid him forever. If she'd wanted to do, it would have been easy. She could have chosen to attend a church outside town, but she wouldn't allow his presence to dictate where she went and didn't go. At least not when it came to church and the only community and people she knew. Claire had resigned herself to the fact that at some point she and Evan would have to speak and function around each other. And why not? They were both adults now and could act as such. More than a decade had passed since they'd parted ways.

Since he'd decided he didn't want her.

An overwhelming wave of sorrow slammed through Claire's chest. Swells of doubt and fear carrying the reminders of all she'd missed out on in life—love, family, dreams. But she was making her own future now, one that didn't depend upon a man. That's how it always should have been.

She let go of Alex and dug her nails into the edge of the shiny counter.

Mrs. Clarkson leaned over the front desk and cleared her throat. "What can I do you for?" Despite living in Goose Harbor for more than forty years, the subtle country twang from her youth hummed through her words from time to time. Mrs. Clarkson was fond of speaking about her childhood in Alabama, although she had never returned after she married, that Claire was aware of.

Claire set her portfolio on the counter and pulled out the application, her letter for the town newsletter detailing her ideas and the petition with the needed signatures. "Just handing these in."

Mrs. Clarkson adjusted her red-framed glasses. A fake diamond sparkled near each temple. "Running for mayor! Oh, how nice. Although—and I mean no offense, dear—but between you and me I sure wish we had an Ashby for our mayor. This town always ran best with someone from that family at the helm." She licked her thumb and used it to flip to the next page. "But there I go. Talking on and on about the old days. Mr. and Mrs. Ashby were both fine mayors—the best— but they are long gone. God rest them both. Do you know that sweet Maggie West still leaves flowers on their graves? Well, but she's Maggie Ashby now, isn't she? She and Kellen do make a pretty pair. Wouldn't it have been wonderful if Kellen was running for office? I find him to be such a kind man. Although, I'm sure you'd do just fine, too."

For more than forty years Henry Ashby had been the mayor of Goose Harbor, and after he passed, his wife, Ida, took over. After her death, Doyle Ellis had been the only one to run for the position. But he'd announced his resignation at the Christmas tree lighting ceremony a few months ago and had sold his house and left town a month later, leaving the position vacant. For now, the head of the town board, Mr. Banks, kept everything running, but everyone knew he wanted out of that responsibility as soon as possible.

Hence the special and rushed election.

Mrs. Clarkson shuffled through the paperwork again, branding each sheet with a Received On stamp bearing the time and date. "Well, now." *Stamp. Stamp.* "It seems we'll have ourselves a real election then, this time around. Don't know how long it's been since we had ourselves one of those. Decades and then some, I think."

"A real election?" Claire closed her portfolio and shoved it back under her arm. "Someone else is running?"

That complicated things some. She'd planned on being the only one on the ballot.

Mrs. Clarkson grinned and nodded. "Why, yes, someone else is running." She held up an application with neat block lettering.

Evan's handwriting.

Claire's stomach performed an impressive somersault before she regrouped, fisting her hand. Hadn't Evan already done enough damage in her life? Well, she wasn't about to let that man steal another one of her dreams.

Claire jerked her head back. "We'll see about that." She grabbed Alex's hand and spun toward the front door, the heels of her boots clicking across the floor.

So today was the day, after all.

It was time to finally have a conversation with the man who'd left her stranded on her wedding day.

Evan flipped up the collar on his coat and then dug around in his pockets for his gloves.

And fine, he was lingering, too.

Claire Atwood had finally spoken to him. Sure, it hadn't been something kind, but that didn't matter. He'd spent the last year wanting to say hi and ease the awkwardness that pulsed between them, but she'd evaded him every time he'd worked up the nerve to break the silence.

She'd been back in town for more than a year and had gone out of her way to dodge him, to the point of crossing to the other side of the street when she happened to spot him downtown. Not that he blamed her. He *had* left her crying on the steps of the county courthouse.

He didn't deserve her attention, not then and not now.

However, the image was burned into his memory—her in a knee-skimming white dress and her red hair tumbling around her shoulders as she sobbed into her hands—forever there to lance pain and regret through him. It sprang to his mind at the worst moments. Like now. A pressure point causing him to wince, desperately making him want to burst through the double doors of town hall and apologize. Explain. Beg her to forgive him.

But to what aim? All those years ago, her father had been right. Evan had been a small-town boy with no ambitions outside of Goose Harbor. He was simple, whereas Claire had possessed big dreams, and she was smart. Brilliant. Evan had heard through the very active Goose Harbor grapevine that Claire had accomplished a lot since their failed wedding. Unless the gossip was mistaken, she'd earned her doctorate and had traveled abroad, studying art history. If they'd married, that never would have happened. Evan would have held her back. He wasn't good enough for her, not then and not now. Even he knew that.

Still, it had hurt to walk away. He wished she at least knew that part.

Evan focused on putting his gloves on. Flexed his hands a few times but still couldn't get his feet to go forward.

The ship that was his future with Claire had sailed many, many years ago. Sailed and sunk like one of the many abandoned boats that lined the bottom of Lake Michigan. If Claire had wanted to discuss their past she wouldn't have disappeared for more than a decade. She wouldn't have hopped on a plane the same day as their failed wedding ceremony. He'd sent notes to her by way of her mother and had never heard back. He hadn't known any of her new information—address, phone number, email address—but most of *his* hadn't changed. She could have called and demanded answers at any point.

But she hadn't.

Truth was, Claire had narrowly missed destroying her life that day, and she probably knew it. The day Evan regretted most was no doubt the biggest relief of her life. No matter what she had thought she felt for him at eighteen years old, it was painfully obvious that she didn't feel anything warm toward him now. So much the better.

She deserved more than being shackled to a Daniels.

Though he'd admit to anyone she looked pretty today. Since returning from New York she often strutted around town too polished, too fancy, wearing designer everything— using her exterior to keep people at a distance the same as she had in their old days together.

Today, though, she'd been flustered because of Alex. The kelly green coat she wore had been buttoned lopsided, the delicate point of her nose was red and winter's breeze had run telltale fingers through her hair, leaving the long auburn strands tangled and dusted with snowflakes.

He didn't know if he'd ever seen her more beautiful.

We haven't talked in twelve years. Let's not start now.

Yup, eleven years of her in New York, and the past year she'd spent in Goose Harbor avoiding him. Her math was sound, and the implications drove nails through any last hopes he might have clung to of them ever getting along again.

The memory of her words pierced his thoughts, leaving his throat suddenly dry. Evan dug farther into his coat pocket for a cough drop. He popped it into his mouth and let the menthol pour through his sinuses. Took a deep breath. Started to leave.

"Wait!" Claire's voice stopped him.

Evan swung around. Sure enough, Claire was stepping toward him at a fast clip, Alex jogging behind her. Her heels hit a slick spot on the narrow path to the town hall and she started to tip backward.

"Whoa." Evan dived forward, quickly slipping his arms around her waist and preventing her from tumbling to the hard ground. His hands came flush against her back, cradling her toward him. Why had he put his gloves on? He would have enjoyed the feel of her hair draped over the back of his hands one more time…

Alex whooped. "Good catch!" Then he bent down, scrambling to collect all Claire's scattered paperwork.

During the process of almost falling, she'd dropped the thick folder-type thing she'd been clutching, and had grabbed on to the lapels of his coat for dear life. Inches from him— close enough to count the freckles she tried to hide—Claire's soft blue eyes frantically moved over his face until their gazes finally met. She sucked in a sharp breath but didn't shove away. His heart pounded like a Sawzall, and just like that he was eighteen again with the woman he had loved in his arms. The woman he had wanted to spend every day of the rest of his life with.

You'll hold her back, son. You'll be a weight around her neck. She'll grow to hate you. Is that what you want? If you love her like you say you do, then let go. It was the first—and more than likely, the only—time he and Sesser Atwood would ever agree so wholeheartedly.

Evan shook that thought away and focused. "I got you."

Smooth, Evan. State the obvious. Women adore that.

"I don't want you to," she whispered. Then her eyes snapped to life and she pushed against his chest.

Ah, right, there it was. The resentment he usually saw setting her features.

Evan let his arms fall away. He swallowed the last of his cough drop, savoring the burning feeling of it going down his throat, grounding him. With her standing nearby, having called to him, he finally summoned the courage to start the conversation he wished he'd had back before she ran to New York City. Might as well get the awkwardness over with. "Claire, this is long overdue, but I need to—"

"Why are you running for mayor?" She crossed her arms over her chest and tapped out a Morse code message detailing her annoyance with the toe of her pointed glossy boot.

Not what he'd expected. Then again, Mrs. Clarkson was known for spreading everyone's business around, in a kindly, grandmotherly way, of course. Claire probably went in to hand over a payment for her family's water or refuse bill, and Mrs. Clarkson couldn't help but tell her all about Evan submitting his application to get on the ballot and run at the final hour.

He scratched the spot where his neck met his jaw. "Oh, that. I guess, why not? The position's open."

And because he and his brother Brice planned to use his clout as mayor to help get a new boatyard and dock built. One that would give Sesser Atwood a run for his money and loosen the chokehold monopoly he had on the shipping business in Goose Harbor. On all businesses in town.

A political tidbit Evan hardly needed to share with the tycoon's daughter.

"That's it?" More toe tapping. A nervous habit he recognized from the old days. Back when he'd known what every single movement she made meant. Known that if her shoulders slumped a certain way she'd had a bad weekend with her parents or an argument with her father. Before she gave a presentation or speech in class, she used to tap her foot faster than his 18-volt jigsaw running on the highest setting.

Evan pointed down and didn't even fight

the smirk he felt tugging at his lips. "You're going to wear out your shoe doing that, you know. Not much is different, huh?"

She stopped and shifted her weight. Narrowed her eyes, and her stare went hard. "*Everything* is different. And don't change the subject."

If looks could kill… The set of her shoulders and jaw told him she was ready for battle. With her expression of fury and her red hair fanned over her shoulders while fat snowflakes fell between them, she looked like a snow queen ready to save her kingdom from an invading army. Sparks and quips made up her favorite line of defense, but he wasn't intimidated. Claire survived by keeping people at a distance, by making them believe she was all burrs and thorns.

Too bad he knew better.

Break through her barriers and she became the sweetest, most sincere person he'd ever met. Her rigid exterior was nothing more than a wall for a terrified girl to hide her heart behind. She only needed someone to cheer her on and infuse some courage into her, something neither of her parents had ever done. At least…that's how she'd been twelve years ago.

In the past, the best way to reach over her

wall was to act like her glares had no effect on him.

"So what if I'm running?" Evan slipped his hands into his pockets and gave an exaggerated shrug. "Why do you care?"

Alex handed Claire the padded folder, which he'd jammed all her papers into, so they stuck out at odd angles. "She wants to know because she's running, too."

"You're running?" Evan rocked forward. "But you don't even *like* this place."

Her eyebrows shot up. "That's so not true." She jabbed her pointer finger in his direction. "And don't you dare say that on the campaign trail. You have no proof to back up your claim."

"Campaign trail? Tell me you're not serious." She was joking...wasn't she? Evan hadn't planned to do much besides getting on the ballot. Everyone in town already knew him.

Alex chuckled. "She is always serious. I know this is a fact."

Evan winked at Alex. He enjoyed how the kid phrased things.

Claire pressed a hand to Alex's chest, as if Evan's very presence might tarnish the boy. She must not be aware that Evan hung out with her son every Sunday. Maybe he should tell her the reason he'd been asked to help out in the seven-and eight-year-old class was because Toby and Jenna Holcomb didn't know how to reach her often angry son. So far, he and Alex had come to a tentative friendship, but her mama-arm protective grab on Alex didn't bode well for Evan's continued involvement.

"See? You have nothing to say," Claire said. "No proof that I don't like this place and no reason why you should continue your run for office."

"No proof? Now let's see… How about you left our humble harbor without so much as looking back, and were gone for more than eleven years? You can't like Goose Harbor all that much—not enough to want to be the mayor—if you didn't even want to be here."

She leaned closer, her voice low, rumbling. "I like Goose Harbor fine."

Evan leaned in, too. "Not as much as you seemed to like New York."

Her eyes flashed. "The reason I left wasn't because I didn't like it here."

"Yeah?" He cocked his head, challenging her. They'd always known how to press each other's buttons. Evidently that much hadn't changed, either. "Then why'd you leave?"

Claire's lips pulled a little. "I left because I didn't like *you*."

Alex's mouth dropped open. "My friend Kasey would call that a burn."

And she'd be right.

Evan filled his chest with a lungful of air and then another. Growing up with an abusive father had taught him to rein in his anger and his reactions, not to speak when he felt wounded, because usually what he had to say only worsened the situation. And to process through the reasons someone would behave a certain way before letting words rule his emotions.

With Claire, it wasn't as if it was a mystery. From her perspective he'd entirely misused her. For all intents and purposes, he'd abandoned her. And she was right, even if it stung. She'd left because of him.

I saved you from a life of regret. You wouldn't have a relationship with your parents if we'd married. You'd probably hate me by now for getting in the way of your dreams.

Why couldn't she understand?

He worked his jaw back and forth.

Someone flung the town hall's doors open. Alex, Evan and Claire all pivoted.

Mr. Banks—also known as the local curmudgeon—bustled toward them. He wore his dress pants up past his belly button and had the bottom of his tie tucked in. No coat, so he must have been in a hurry. Wisps from his comb-over rose to stand on end in the winter wind. The man currently served—begrudgingly—as the stand-in mayor, and grumbled about it to anyone who would listen.

Mr. Banks puffed when he reached them. "You're both still here. Good."

Evan relaxed his shoulders and forced himself to put mental space between the conversation with Mr. Banks and the confrontation with Claire. "Is there a problem with our applications?"

"No. They'll do. I'd like you both to attend the board meeting on Tuesday so I can introduce each of you to the public."

Evan glanced at Claire and then back at Mr. Banks. "Is that necessary? I'm pretty sure everyone voting already knows us."

"It's a formality," the stand-in mayor huffed.

Evan bit back a laugh. He coughed once and then cleared his throat. "And this is Goose Harbor—hardly the place for formalities."

Mr. Banks scowled. "Are you certain you're qualified for this office, Mr. Daniels?"

Claire stepped forward. "I was just trying to talk him out of it, too!"

Mr. Banks narrowed his eyes at them. "To rise to the needs of the position of mayor, I hope you're both going to start caring about formalities and acting professionally." He smoothed his hand down his bright orange tie. "Our town deserves that from their elected."

"Of course." Claire bristled. "I only meant—"

Mr. Banks cut her off with a deep frown. "We need to discuss when is best for both of you regarding the board of trustees planning the competitive events for this election."

"Excuse me?" Claire wrapped her arms around Alex and pulled him to stand in front of her like a human shield.

"I'm with her." Evan jutted his thumb. "What do you mean by *competitive events*?"

Mr. Banks groaned and shook his head. "Pie eating contests, fund-raising, talent shows. Some or other manner of horrible sorts of things like that. You know how this town is."

"We're running for mayor." Chill painted red across Claire's cheeks. "Not a pageant title."

Evan chuckled, trying to lighten her mood.

"And if we were, it's awful cold for a swimsuit competition, not that I'd turn one down."

She twisted toward him. "How do you expect anyone to actually vote for you? You can't be serious for even three minutes. It's unbelievable."

Alex spun in his mom's arms. "He can, too. You should hear him at Sunday school. He talks about God better than any of the Atwoods do."

Claire gripped Alex by the shoulder, snagging her son's attention. "Don't forget, you're an Atwood, too."

He shrugged and pushed out of her reach. "Must be why I don't really know God at all."

Mr. Banks worked his jaw. "It's cold out here, and if you haven't noticed, my coat's still inside. This was *supposed* to be a quick conversation."

"Apologies." Claire plastered on a smile. "Continue."

"Per the town's charter, those running for mayor must take part in friendly competitions."

Evan brought his fist to his mouth and cleared his throat again. "I guess the thing that has us confused is we've never done that with an election in the past. I've lived here my whole life and I've never heard any of this."

Mr. Banks closed his eyes for a moment and shook his head slightly, as if Evan and Claire were gnats buzzing by his ears. "We haven't had more than one person running for mayor in a long time." He shivered and made as if he was about to leave, but then added, "I'm moving up the election, too. It'll be the second week of March."

Claire's mouth opened, closed, opened again. "But that's…that's only a little more than a month away."

"I suggest you get to campaigning." Mr. Banks scooted backward, in the direction of the entranceway. "I'll contact you both with the date and details for the first event. I assume weekends and evenings work best?"

They both nodded.

Evan dug in his pockets, searching for another cough drop, but found nothing.

"This ridiculousness can't be done soon enough for me," Mr. Banks said. "May the best person win."

"Thanks." Claire hugged her folder. "I intend to."

Alex waved at Evan while Claire tugged her son toward the car. Evan watched them leave before heading to his heavy-duty truck. "What did I just get myself into?"

Chapter Two

"You can do this. It'll be no different than talking to anyone else," Claire coached herself, occasionally glancing into her car's rearview mirror as she drove across town. Gray clouds crowded together and rolled over each other in the sky like a group of children pushing toward the promise of free ice cream. They were making their way over Lake Michigan, directly toward her. Goose Harbor was in for another round of lake effect snow.

Good. A pending storm was the perfect excuse. That gave her a reason to keep the visit short.

Visit.

That was hardly the right word.

Since being home, Claire had made a point of never driving past Evan's house. Not a difficult task considering he lived in the thick, wooded area on the far reaches of the town's limits—almost in the unincorporated section that belonged to the county. Claire rarely had a need to head out in that direction, and even if she did, there were roads she could take to bypass the stretch of land she knew he owned.

Now it all felt silly. She'd mentally blown this moment—contact with Evan initiated by her—way out of proportion.

Why had she let a person from her past, someone she hadn't uttered a word to in more than a decade, have that sort of control on her life? She'd gotten over Evan a long time ago. He was an immature mistake. Falling for a cute guy had been an understandable blunder on the cusp of adulthood. She'd met plenty of people in college with far bigger regrets. So she'd entertained the idea of running off with her high school boyfriend, getting married at the county courthouse? It hadn't happened.

Good, again.

She glanced in the rearview mirror another time. Dark storm clouds bubbled behind her. She'd focus on the *behind her* part. The path ahead of her was known, easy. Goose Harbor, her family, working for her father—she could have a life here. And the past was just that, the past. It couldn't harm her any longer.

And yet her hands were trembling on the steering wheel.

"He has no power over me. None."

Sure, she'd mourned their relationship, and the question *Why wasn't I good enough?* still lingered. But it wasn't as if she'd spent years pining after him. Claire had moved on a long time ago, which was why she'd been able to get engaged to Auden Pierce, the most sought-after solutions architect for Fortune 500 companies, two years ago. At the stop sign she glanced down at her bare left ring finger and sighed. She'd called off the wedding six months in advance, leaving Auden speechless at first—not an easy feat—but at least she'd given him warning long before the day of the ceremony.

Unlike Evan.

Before she left Goose Harbor for college, Evan had still lived with his parents on a run-down piece of parched land that her father rented to the Danielses. Evan's dad had been forever behind on payments, but her father had never kicked them out, though he'd threatened it many times. Often Mom would blow up and yell about the Danielses at family dinners, but Dad had always talked her off the ledge. He'd explained to Claire that it was their "Godly duty" to help out the *unfortunate.* Oddly, it was the only time Dad had ever been remotely spiritually minded or seemed to care about people who were in a different tax bracket than the Atwoods.

Curiosity about the Danielses had bloomed in Claire at a young age, probably because of her parents' heated fights over the family. When she'd finally rubbed shoulders with Evan in classes during freshman year of high school, she'd hung back, studied him. Evan had been one of those students who commanded the classroom with a funny remark and a winning smile. He'd strutted the hallways, high-fiving upperclassmen while a flood of followers trailed after him. As a teenager, he'd always been smiling, joking and full of confidence. While he hadn't been a jock or among the top tier of popular kids, he'd been well liked by everyone.

Her father's word—*unfortunate*—had never fitted Evan's brothers, Brice and Andrew, either. He had a younger sister, too, but Claire didn't know Laura well.

Over the years Claire had grown to despise that word *unfortunate.*

Who decided the merits of a fortunate person versus an unfortunate one? Were finances all that mattered when applying the label? It was one of those words that, when used by someone in good economic standing to describe others, felt like a pat to the speaker's back and an insult to the one being described. In her social circles, especially among her Christian friends, she'd heard it a hundred times since her father had first uttered the word.

"Let's organize a fund-raiser to help those unfortunate children without clean water in Africa."

"I saw this homeless man on the side of the road with a sign—how unfortunate."

"For our outreach project let's do a food drive for the unfortunate."

"Did you see the viral story about that unfortunate puppy who was born without hind legs?"

Fact was, in high school, when Claire had first observed Evan, she had come to the conclusion that *she* was the unfortunate one, not him. He could sway a crowd with a fast quip. He was surrounded by friends. He charmed the principal and every teacher he came into contact with. However, Claire had walked the halls with her books tightly pressed to her chest and chin to her collarbone. If her father had known how timid she'd been around her peers he would have been disappointed in her.

She'd slunk to the back of the classroom and lost her voice when the teacher called on her.

Up to that point freshman year, she hadn't made one real friend in her whole life. Not one her own age.

Not until Evan.

Claire hooked the hand she wasn't using for driving onto her shoulder and pulled at her tight muscles. She sucked in a deep breath and held it for the mental count of three, then let it out. She repeated the breathing exercise for the next mile.

What she and Evan had during high school hadn't been real friendship, either. Because friends don't walk away like he did, at least, not the type of friends she'd always imagined having. Perhaps that's why she still had such a difficult time connecting with people her age and always felt so out of place when she had to make small talk. Claire was definitely the unfortunate one. Money had nothing to do with it.

"Stop. You have friends. Kendall is your friend. There. See? That's plenty," Claire muttered as she turned onto the street that led past Crest Orchard, where Jenna and Toby Holcomb lived. The couple's daughter, Kasey, was Alex's best friend.

She took the tight curve extra slowly, remembering the car accident last year that had claimed the life of the community's young pastor. The town had installed a wide guardrail to prevent cars from skidding off the road and going down the cliff that hung over Lake Michigan, but slow and steady was probably still the best course of action.

Her father's voice rang in her ears. *Atwoods don't back down. Losers back down, and Atwoods are winners. We settle for nothing less. You remember that.*

She straightened her shoulders and lifted her chin. "I can do this."

Dense woods hugged either side of the road. After a slight bend, Claire passed the dirt patch of a clearing that she knew, because of her friendship with Kendall, led to Brice Daniels's cabin. Claire had actually had dinner at Brice's house a handful of times in the last few months to help with planning their wedding. She was Kendall's maid of honor, after all.

She worked her fingers into the leather of her steering wheel. Evan's land butted up to Brice's. The brothers had purchased the land together when a piece of the old summer camp had gone on the market. They'd divided the land between them and each had built a home.

More than likely she was driving by some of Evan's property right now. Half a mile later, she found Evan's wide concrete driveway, just as Kendall had described. A large sage-colored Craftsman home sat on the curved part of the U-shaped driveway. Claire eased her car into Park. The front of the house boasted a welcoming terrace-style porch with a swing on one end and a set of red rocking chairs on the other. Everything about it spoke of warmth and comfort.

Looks could be deceiving.

Still, she'd be the first to admit that he'd obviously done well for himself over the years. He had a home and a successful life here in their hometown. His handmade furniture graced many of the houses and shops in Goose Harbor. But Claire had found success, too; it only looked different. An undergraduate degree from Columbia University was nothing to sneeze at, and her master's from Sotheby's Institute of Art wasn't too shabby, either. Her parents still griped about her "worthless" degrees—an undergraduate in visual arts, master's in art business and a PhD in art history—however, they were proud of the fact that her studies had taken her to London, Hong Kong and Shanghai. The list went on. She had no reason to feel less than when compared to her high school boyfriend.

She gulped down any remaining doubt. She needed to speak with him—needed to convince him to join her in an attempt to talk the board of trustees out of making her and Evan go through a circus act of friendly competitions. If they approached the board together they had a better chance of getting a pass on the very dated town tradition. She couldn't go to the board on her own without the risk of appearing to be a spoilsport.

Claire tucked her keys into her purse and then ran a hand over her hair. "Evan Daniels, ready or not, here I come."

Evan paced around the stone-topped island in his kitchen, cell phone pressed to his ear while he waited for Brice to pick up. His brother was hit or miss about answering, but Evan would keep calling tonight until he did. They had to readjust their plan.

Brice answered on the third ring. "If you're trying to talk me out of more of my venison steaks, the answer is no."

Evan fought a grin. "Tempting, but not why I called."

"I know you used my spare key and took some out of my freezer last week." Brice's voice held a teasing tone. "I hid the key some-where else. You'll have to search harder next time."

Brice had two hiding spots for the key. He wouldn't move it somewhere beyond those places. That's one of the things Evan really liked about his brother—he was steady, de-pendable, predictable. Evan looked up to him. Brice was more than his older brother and friend; he was somewhat of a mentor, too.

But sentimental conversations tended to make Brice uncomfortable. Evan would keep the conversation to facts and the occasional ribbing, even if he would have liked to say something…deeper.

"What's mine is yours, brother."

"You're fortunate I like you. And you said that wrong. You meant what's yours is mine." Brice…joking? Meeting Kendall Mayes and getting engaged had really changed his brother. For the better. His introverted sibling now had a goofy side. He smiled more. See-ing the positive changes in Brice was almost enough to make Evan wish he hadn't given up on romantic relationships.

Almost.

Relationships might work for someone like Brice, who deserved to be happy, but not Evan. He'd allowed the people he cared about to get hurt, some of them many times. He wasn't a strong protector like Brice. He'd only end up disappointing a woman.

Evan shoved those thoughts away and focused on the conversation again. "Have you bothered to look in the freezer since Friday? I already replaced them."

"You always do. That's why I keep you around."

While he enjoyed laughing with his brother, it was time to get to the topic at hand. Evan stopped walking and braced his hand on the countertop. "We need to talk."

Brice chuckled on the other end. "Sounds ominous."

"It's bad, Brice."

"You do know there are only a few weeks left until my wedding. Maybe we can save bad news until after then? All the last-minute details are stressing Kendall out—which means they're stressing me out, too."

"I'm sorry, but it can't wait." Evan inched toward the row of bar stools he kept tucked under the overhang on the kitchen island, pulled one out and sat down.

Brice sighed. "Hit me with it, then."

"Turns out I'm not the only one running for mayor."

"But I thought you handed in your application at the last minute? We called this morning and there was no one else."

Evan looked down at his hand. "Well, there is now."

"Who?"

"Claire."

"Atwood?"

Evan let out an exasperated laugh. "Is there another?"

Brice grumbled something low and unintelligible. Exactly the response Evan had figured.

"What am I going to do?" He snagged a pen from where it rested next to a bowl of fruit, flipped over an old church bulletin and started sketching a plan for a playground that he'd been contracted to build at the Holcombs' apple orchard.

"Simple. Beat her in the election."

His pen froze. "You think I should still run?"

"Of course you should still run. You have to."

Evan clicked the pen a couple times. "You know she'll have Sesser's muscle behind her." And his money—her father was one of the wealthiest men in the state. He owned land and had his hand in businesses all along the shore of Lake Michigan, down into Indiana and on to Chicago. The tycoon might live in a cozy tourist town, but Evan knew not to underestimate the man's power. Or the bite it carried.

Evan still bore the scars from last time he'd crossed paths with Claire's father.

"That could be her greatest disadvantage." Brice talked to someone else for a moment, saying he'd be only a few more seconds—Kendall. "Most people don't trust him. Use that against her."

"I won't run a smear campaign. Not against her." They might not be on friendly terms, but the thought of bad-mouthing Claire publicly turned his stomach. He'd hurt her enough for one lifetime; he wouldn't do it again.

An uncomfortable silence pulsed over the phone line before Brice said, "Don't tell me, after all this time, you still have feelings for her?"

Evan straightened and ran his palm back and forth over his jean-clad thigh. "Let me rephrase that. I wouldn't run a smear campaign against *anyone*. It doesn't matter that it's her. Claire and me? We don't even belong in a sentence together. You know I let that go a long time ago."

"Did you...?" His brother lowered his

voice. "You never told her about Sesser, did you?"

Evan examined the calluses on his hands. Workman's hands. Hands of a blue-collar man who did manual labor for a living and would never be good enough for a woman from Claire's world. "She doesn't need to know."

"It's probably for the best."

"Not probably. It is—was. Everything is how it should be. Needs to be." His voice sounded hollow to his own ears.

"We have to beat her. Understand? No matter what you think about her or if you believe she has good intentions about becoming mayor, it doesn't matter. Sesser will find a way to use her in that position to gain a stronger hold on everything." Brice summed up the reasons that he'd used to talk Evan into running in the first place. "You and I both know that's what'll happen. You're running to take back some power from him—so we can build a dock and remove his monopoly. We can't give Sesser another foothold."

"I guess you're right." Evan kept clicking the pen.

"He'd ruin this town. He'd use her to turn this place into somewhere we wouldn't want to live. You get that, don't you?"

"True." *Click. Click. Click.* "I wouldn't put anything past Sesser."

That was the reason *Brice* had urged him to run, but in truth, Evan had decided to go for it because he cared about the people in Goose Harbor and wanted to fight for their best interests. Maybe the two were the same thing. Brice was the more levelheaded brother— the one who turned ideas over and looked at something from every angle before deciding the best course of action. Whereas Evan often found himself in hot water because of split-second choices that he hadn't stopped and thought through. He'd trust his brother on this. On everything.

The doorbell rang, making Evan slide off of the stool. "Someone's here. I gotta go."

"If it's that boy for Laura again—"

"Don't worry, papa bear, I've got it handled." Evan clicked off and set his phone on the counter. Brice had a tendency to be overprotective with all the siblings, although he'd gained the right to be that way after protecting Evan, Andrew and Laura as best an eldest brother could during childhood.

Their seventeen-year-old sister had moved in with Evan soon after Brice and Kendall had become engaged last summer. Brice had tried to talk Laura into remaining at his place, assuring her it was fine to stay until he and Kendall returned from their honeymoon, but Laura had still chosen to head to Evan's. Their parents' house was no longer a fit environment for their teenage sister, not that it had ever been an ideal place to begin with. Growing up, Dad had physically abused Brice and had lobbed verbal assaults at the rest of them, Laura included. And their mother had become a bitter hoarder over the years, turning the small house into something of a health code hazard.

Besides, Evan's home was bigger than Brice's. His older brother lived in a cabin with one bedroom, which Laura had used while Brice had camped out in his office area for a couple months. Evan had three bedrooms and a fully finished basement. Laura had plenty of space to invite friends over or have parties here, where she hadn't been able to be very social when she lived with Brice. And Evan never minded company. He thrived off it, whereas Brice was introverted, and even having their sister stay had been a strain on him.

It was better this way.

"Laura," Evan hollered from the bottom of the stairs. "Are you expecting anyone?"

No answer. She probably couldn't hear him

over the loud Broadway tunes blasting from her room. She had aspirations for a life in the theater and was starring in the high school's production of *The Music Man* this year. In the last few weeks he'd listened to her belting out "Goodnight, My Someone" and "Till There Was You" too many times to count.

Evan shook his head as he crossed to the front entryway. If it was the boy who'd been pursuing Laura since the summer, Evan would let him in. Laura was growing into a smart young woman; she could navigate her relationships without one of her brothers acting like a domineering father. He'd give her advice, of course—and stay within earshot—but he wouldn't shove away a guy unless she asked him to.

However, Evan didn't find a lanky teen on the other side of the door.

He found Claire Atwood.

Chapter Three

Claire bunched the handles of her purse together. Relaxed her fingers. Wound the straps around her hands again.

She took a glance over her shoulder as she shot out a long stream of air. Dark clouds scudded across the sky behind her, rolling closer. *Good.* If a blizzard started, it wouldn't be fun to drive through, but they needed it. Perhaps the ground would stay cold enough that the fresh covering would stick around for the next two weeks, lasting for Valentine's weekend.

Maybe she'd wear black and protest the holiday. Claire bit back a smile. Of course she'd never do something like that, especially when she was running for mayor, but it was still fun to imagine doing so.

She ran her fingers over her hair, trying

to put back into place strands the wind had moved. If Evan didn't answer before she counted to twenty, she'd head home. Because she shouldn't have come here, shouldn't have showed up without calling first. The website for his woodworking business probably had a Contact Me section where she could have located a phone number or an email address. No doubt Mrs. Clarkson or Kendall had his information, but asking either would have encouraged too many questions and unwanted speculation.

He probably wasn't even home. Evan's outgoing personality assured he had a busy social schedule, or at least Claire assumed so.

The door swung open and she sucked in a sharp breath.

Evan was home, all right.

Wearing worn jeans and a white T-shirt, he stood barefoot in the doorway, his lips slightly parted. "What are you—? Why are—? I don't und—?" He shook his head and took a step to the side, sweeping his hand in a grand welcoming motion. "Come in. Please, it's freezing out there."

Right; go into his house. She hadn't thought that far ahead. Had she thought at all? After dropping Alex off for a sleepover at his friend Xander's, she had gotten into her car and turned it in the direction of Evan's house. Despite the fact that they hadn't spoken in years, she'd known she had to talk with him now and needed to do so before her courage waned.

Of course they'd talk inside—it was far too cold to stand outside for long. And thinking she was only dropping Alex off at his sleepover and driving back home, she hadn't chosen to wear her warmest coat.

She hugged her purse to her stomach and stepped past Evan. He reached behind her and closed the door, bringing him a little closer as he did so. She backed away, finding his arm only inches from her side. His hair was tousled, as if he'd been tugging on it. A waft of the watermelon scent hit her and she turned away.

But she couldn't turn off the images the smell made rush into her mind.

When they were teenagers, she used to love watching him work out a problem. Evan would sit at a table, transfixed on a piece of paper, gnawing on a pencil as he tried to sketch whatever he was planning to build next. Sometimes she had curled up beside him at the library or scratched his back as he worked. Other times she had slung her legs over his and hugged his side, her head burrowed into his chest as she memorized the steady pounding of his heartbeat while he stretched to reach the paper. Whenever he got stuck, he'd absentmindedly shove a hand into his hair and yank so that by the time his drawing was complete his hair would be sticking up in all directions.

She used to love how completely absorbed he became when he was dreaming, thinking, building. How he'd been the kind of person who threw his entire being into a project. They'd fantasized about attending college together, as a married couple, supporting each other as they took their time with their studies. Evan's plan had been to study engineering, but she'd learned from Kendall that he had never ended up leaving Goose Harbor.

Shunning all thoughts of Evan Daniels had become such a habit for Claire that it was difficult to sort through the sudden onslaught of memories. They felt like talons, piercing her heart with burst after burst of pain. A tight coil of ache wrapped around her ribs. She pressed her palm into her collarbone.

Evan scooted so he was standing in front of her, then scratched the back of his neck. "You okay?"

"Fine." Being ridiculous...but she was fine. For all intents and purposes, Evan was basically a stranger. She no longer knew the man before her, and there was no logical reason to be affected by him.

Still, it was dangerous to dwell on the past. "I'm fine," she repeated.

"Good. That's great." He rocked on his feet and glanced at the impressive fire blazing in the stone fireplace in his family room. A log cracked and hissed. "I mean, I'm glad you're fine."

Claire hooked a chunk of her hair between her fingers and put it back behind her ear, casually scanning the layout of Evan's home as she did so. The entryway was spacious, with a ceiling that reached to the second story. Behind a half wall there was a large family room with an overstuffed couch and two wide lounge chairs. Ten feet past the entryway lay the stairs; the railing and posts were clearly Evan's handiwork. Beyond was a dining room and an open kitchen with gleaming appliances and a huge island. A set of white French doors led to another room that she couldn't make out.

All the areas she could see were splashed in soothing earth tones. The aesthetics of Evan's house translated to an overwhelming message to come on in, take a seat, relax, stay.

Well, everything except the loud music

booming from upstairs. Claire pointed toward the steps. "When did you get into show tunes?"

Evan barked out a laugh. "Not me. No. That's Laura. My sister. Do you remember her?"

"She was little." Claire held her hand at waist height. "When I…when I was last around."

"Not so little anymore. She's seventeen," he offered. "She pretty much lives here."

Claire wanted to ask why his teenage sister lived with him. Were his parents here, too? His brother Andrew? No, the local rumor mill had hinted that Evan's younger brother had run off six or seven years ago and no one knew if he was dead or alive. Some of the gossip was that Andrew had gone to Vegas and fallen into gambling like his father, but others told a tale of him becoming a world traveler, backpacking through India. Whatever his story, it no longer sounded as if it was entwined with Evan's. However, none of that mattered. The less she knew about Evan's life now, the better.

"You've done well for yourself." Claire gestured to encompass his whole house. "Your place is beautiful."

Evan ducked his head and glanced around.

He looked slightly unsure. "Claire, listen. This is awkward." He scrubbed his hand over his jaw. "But it doesn't have to be."

Both of them running for mayor *was* awkward, but they were adults and could deal with it. She sucked in a fortifying breath. Now or never. "We need to talk."

He took a tentative step closer. "I know— I'm sorry. There's a lot I've wanted to say." His hand came up, as if he wanted to take her hand, or hug her, or rest it on her shoulder, but just as quickly he let it drop to his side. He shook his head once. "You have no idea how sorry I am. About everything."

Danger! The conversation was not going in the right direction whatsoever. The last thing she wanted was to dig up and rehash any part of their old relationship. She'd held a funeral and buried those lost hopes a long time ago. Exhuming the grave was not going to happen. Not on her watch.

Evan's brow pinched. "I've always re—"

She held up her palm. "I don't want to talk about *that*. That's nòt why I came here."

"But I still—"

"No," she said, louder and with more force than she meant to. "I'm serious. Please. I don't want to go down that road with you.

Not now, not ever." She tugged on one of her sleeves. "Understood?"

He nodded. "I can respect that." Then he swallowed hard. "If that's what you want."

It was strange to see the ever-sure Evan off-kilter and subdued. Maybe he'd changed over the years. Then again, he could be unnerved about being alone with her. At eighteen he'd decided he never wanted to be with her, and now he was stuck in such a predicament, if only for a few minutes.

Unwanted. Unwelcome. Undesirable.

Not much had changed in twelve years.

She needed to stop thinking like that.

Evan narrowed his eyes. "Wait, you're not here to try to convince me to drop out of the race, are you?" He stepped back, leaned against the half wall that separated his entryway from the living room and crossed his arms over his chest. "That's not happening, no matter what you say. I hope you know that."

She rolled her shoulders. Sparring with Evan was far more comfortable than where the conversation had almost gone.

"Oh, believe me, if you're as cocky and mule-headed as you were in high school, then of course you're not going to back down." She set her purse on the half wall's ledge. "So no, I'm not here to ask you to drop out."

The confident smirk she remembered from the past returned to his face. "Cocky and mule-headed, huh? I seem to remember running for president of the senior class and winning."

"Thank you for demonstrating my point."

He rolled his eyes in mock annoyance, but the tug of a smile hinted that he was enjoying their quick exchange.

"Besides," Claire added, "you won because I didn't run against you." The words came out weak in her ears. If she had run against Evan back then no one would have voted for her. Evan was her best friend and she had a group of friends based on that, but she'd had none to call her own when she was a teenager. Fellow students had either been afraid of her, because of her father, or tried to befriend her in order to get something—again, because of her father.

"Hey!" Evan's twin dimples appeared as he wagged his finger. "I won fair and square."

Thank you for not taking a cheap shot.

"Oh right, completely fair." A genuine laugh sneaked out. "Is *that* what you call flirting for every vote?"

"I did not—"

She let out a little *eep*. "You're planning to get votes that way this time, too, aren't you? Don't deny it. You'll bat your eyes and 'yes, ma'am' and hold doors all around town for every woman over thirty and get them all swooning."

"One." He pushed off the wall so he was standing less than two feet away. It felt too close, but her back was already against the door and she had nowhere to go. "Last I checked, being polite and respectful isn't considered flirting. Two." He used his fingers to tick off his points. "I didn't win the high school election by flirting. We were dating. You probably don't think very highly of me, and I've earned the lowest marks in your book with cause." He shoved his hand into his hair and turned to the side. "But know that I'm never going to—how did you say it?" He met her gaze and Claire swallowed past the burn in her throat. "*Bat my eyes* at another woman if I'm committed to someone else. Three, for that matter I don't think I even know what batting my eyes means. And four—"

She held up both her hands. "Okay, enough."

"Four." He cocked his head and his dimples deepened. "You think I can make women all over town swoon?"

And...he's back.

This time she didn't fight the smile that bloomed on her face. "Grow up."

"You're the one who suggested it." He tapped his chin in an exaggerated manner. "Actually, the idea has merit."

"Don't pretend you have no clue what I'm talking about. I've heard the rumors."

"What rumors?" His face fell.

"About how *friendly*—" she put the word in finger quotes "—you are with the tourists."

He looked genuinely confused. "I guess I don't understand what you're insinuating."

Come on, he had to know. A guy as good-looking as he was had to comprehend the effect he had on a single woman if he was showering her with attention. "Please, Evan. Don't play stupid."

"Are you kidding?" His confusion melted into a goofy grin as he pointed at his face. "This is what *real* stupid looks like. Take a picture. You might be able to sell it to the Discovery Channel. *'Stupid, Captured in the Wild.'*" He imitated a voice-over from an animal documentary.

"You're impossible."

He finally sobered. "Whatever you've heard, I don't flirt with anyone. At least, not on purpose. I haven't even had a girlfriend since..." He shrugged.

Since when? Since her? That would be impossible. A guy like Evan would be considered a hot commodity in a small town like Goose Harbor. Grandmas would invite their adult granddaughters to visit for the summer just to try to pair them up with him. An eligible, attractive bachelor who was deeply involved in the community and his church— what wasn't to like?

Too bad when Claire looked at him she saw promise-breaker, dream-dasher and leaver, but she was in tune enough to understand why others might be drawn to him.

Evan studied her for a minute, almost as if he wanted to say something important. Finally, he shook his head and said, "Forgive me, where are my manners? Here." He held out a hand. "I'll take your coat. It's cold out there. Let's go sit by the fire and we can discuss whatever it was you wanted to."

Evan crossed from the kitchen to the couch near the fireplace where Claire waited. The smell of chocolate from the mugs in his hands and the burning logs that popped and crackled in the hearth should have been comforting, but he was finding it impossible to relax.

Claire Atwood was in his house.

Years had come and gone since he'd given up hope of them reconciling, so that couldn't be what was causing his pulse to heat the back of his neck. Long ago, Evan had been told he'd never amount to anything. His father had been the first to plant the idea in his head, but many others had reinforced the notion until it became true.

Out of everything Sesser Atwood had said to Evan to convince him to miss his own wedding—between the blackmail about kicking his parents out of their home, having his father arrested, and Sesser's promise to use his connection to get Brice tossed out of college—it wasn't the threats that had convinced Evan to abandon Claire in the end. It was the reminder that Evan would never amount to anything, never be good enough to deserve someone of Claire's stature. He'd been no better than a pauper with a crush on a princess. Laughable.

Sesser had been right.

While Evan had gone on to build a home in Goose Harbor, he'd never ventured beyond the small lakeside community. With no college degree, he had nothing to attach to his name and very little experience in the world at large. All he had to show for his life was the furniture he built with sweat and dreams. Many of the people he'd grown up with would consider his house to be nice, sizable even, but it was a joke when compared to the place Claire had grown up in. Nothing compared to what Auden Pierce, the man she'd been engaged to, could have given her.

He'd never admit to it, but once he discovered that Claire was engaged, Evan had harbored a fascination for conducting internet searches on her fiancé. Auden Pierce—who looked as stuffy in his online profiles as his name sounded—was her senior by eight years, and newspapers quoted that the solutions architect was worth twice as much as her father. Evan initially had to look up what a solutions architect even was—some fancy term for someone who designs plans for problems occurring within huge corporations. Starting pay was upwards into six figures. Evan had stopped searching for information after learning that.

Then again, some of the articles about Pierce's dealings had sounded shady. Not exactly illegal, but not completely on the up and up...much like how Sesser Atwood ran his businesses. Evan wouldn't survive ten minutes in such a world. He couldn't even let himself beat one of the Sunday school kids at a board game without feeling bad.

Evan and Claire existed in different spheres, and that's how it would always be.

How it needed to be.

He handed her a large mug and then sat on the chair across from the couch, the fire warming the side of his face. "I put peanut butter cups in there. You may want to give it a stir so they don't stay melted on the bottom." He pointed at the mug she had cradled in her hand. "I hope you still like it that way. I should have asked."

Claire stared at the steam rising from her hot chocolate and blinked a couple times. "I—yes—I still love it that way." She slowly stirred the liquid, her spoon making soft clanking sounds. "It's been forever." She took a sip and her eyes softened as she watched him. "I have to start making it this way for Alex. I'd forgotten."

Forgotten her favorite way to take hot chocolate?

Evan wanted to say something, anything that would ease the tension between them, but she'd asked him to not bring up the past. She wanted to forget that they'd ever meant something to each other, which was probably wise, but Evan was struggling with the idea of ignoring the issue all the same. How could they move forward and function together on any level without addressing what had happened? She wanted him to ignore everything? Pretend they'd never known each other? Held each other?

If only she'd let him explain.

Emotion tightened his throat.

Claire placed her mug on the coffee table and put her hands on her knees. "I stopped by because I wanted to talk about the election."

Heat wafted in thick waves from the fireplace. He might have added one too many logs when he built it earlier; then again, he hadn't been planning to sit this close. Evan angled away from it. He rested his ankle on his other knee and cradled his half-empty hot chocolate. "I figured that much."

"This competition they want us to do." She moved to the edge of the seat. "It's ridiculous. Please tell me you think so, too."

Evan chuckled. "Of course it's ridiculous."

"Oh, that's great! I'm so glad you agree." She wound her fingers together around her cup. "So you'll talk to the board about it with me, then? We need to convince them to drop the idea. If only you would talk to them, I know you could get them to see reason."

Ah, the truth came out.

Claire wanted him to address the board, to get her out of doing something she had decided was uncomfortable. The same scenario had played out a hundred times in high school, with Evan always going to bat for her. But not this time. Claire was a grown woman who didn't need him as a mouthpiece. She was smart and well-spoken and strong enough to fight her own battles. Her father might still attempt to hold her under his thumb, but Evan knew better. Even after all these years, he believed in Claire—in the fire and determination he knew she possessed. She lacked courage, not ability.

Evan pressed his shoulders into the chair's padding. "Now, I didn't say I'd do that."

Claire's mouth opened, closed and then opened again. She let out a huff. "But you said you agreed it's ridiculous."

"I do." He finished his drink and then leaned forward and set the mug a few inches under his chair, where it wouldn't get knocked over. Out of habit, he rubbed his hands together. Usually the motion was to clear his skin of sawdust. "I can acknowledge the whole thing is silly and still go along with it."

"Evan, it's…we're not in a beauty pageant here!" Her eyebrows shot up. She clanked her mug onto the coffee table. "All I want is to run a few ads and shake some hands and call it a day. Why can't this just be a normal election?"

"Easy answer." He absently traced a pattern into the suede fabric on the armrest of his chair. "This is Goose Harbor. People here live for traditions and events that bring the community together. Everyone's been stuck in their homes all winter. Some people are worried about making ends meet after a slow tourist season."

Claire nodded. "All true points, but none of that has anything to do with our election."

Evan straightened in the seat. "It has *everything* to do with the election. A fun event to attend gives them hope. If you can't see that, then you really need to rethink your desire to be the mayor here." He leaned forward once more, bracing his elbows on his knees. "Why are you running, Claire? Did your father—"

She shot to her feet. "This has nothing to do with my father. Understand?" She ground out the words. "Why would you even think—? I'm my own person." Claire pressed her palm to her heart. "Out of everyone, I thought you knew that."

"I'm sorry." He hooked his hand around his neck, then ruffled his hair. "I shouldn't have said that."

"Well, it was said and can't be taken back." She rounded the chair and headed for the door. "Nothing can be taken back."

Evan sighed. "I know that better than anyone." He slowly stood, stepped forward and dropped his hand on the edge of the chair. "Why'd you come home, Claire? The truth."

Her back was toward him. He watched her shoulders rise with a deep breath. She had every right to barge out his door without supplying an answer. He wasn't owed one.

Claire fisted her hand and spun around. "Why did *you* stay?"

Not what he was expecting.

Evan rocked on his feet. "I have nowhere else to go."

"Same." One word, but her voice caught on it. "That's the reason I'm here."

Evan started toward her, his feet moving before he could determine if he wanted to comfort her or not. He couldn't leave her standing there, looking like she was about to cry. He had to do something. Given that they were running against each other, and given their past, he probably shouldn't. But logical reasoning had never been his strong suit.

However, it had always been Claire's, which was probably why, before he could make it to her side, she gathered her coat and purse and fumbled with the doorknob. She yanked it open. "I'll see you at the town hall meeting tomorrow." She wrapped her scarf around her neck and flung the end of it over her shoulder, then shoved her arms into her coat. "I'll be the one winning, in case there was still any confusion."

The door slammed before he could take another step. The sound reverberated through his chest and a clump of sadness thudded into the bottom of his gut, the weight reminding him that there was no reason to chase after her. Claire didn't want him to follow; she'd made that clear twelve years ago when he wrote her letter after letter for a year and she never responded.

"Night, Claire," he mumbled.

"Whoa! That lady is a tornado in high heels." Laura pounded down the stairs behind him. When she wasn't lying on the floor of her bedroom listening to music, his sister seemed to always be in a hurry.

Evan gathered the empty mugs from the family room and carried them to the sink. "How much of that did you overhear?"

His sister followed in his wake, then boosted herself onto the island's counter. "You mean, how much of that did I intentionally eavesdrop on from my prime hiding location at the top of the stairs?"

Evan raised an eyebrow at her as he rinsed out the cups. Despite the thirteen-year age gap, he was close to his sister, and he loved her fiercely. The two of them enjoyed ribbing each other as much as he made a habit out of kidding with Brice.

Laura snagged an apple from the fruit bowl and bit into it with a loud crunch. "Oh, only all of it."

"You should wash that before eating it."

"Okay, Mom." She rubbed the apple on her jeans and then took another bite.

"Laura." His voice held a warning. "An ounce of respect would be nice."

It was difficult, this balance between them. He wanted to be her fun-loving brother. Someone she could always tease and be lighthearted with. There was so much heaviness attached to the rest of their family relationships, even with Brice. Evan yearned to make sure she knew she could be herself with him—even if that meant sassing him occasionally. Yet he was left to play parent as well, which often carried the weight of setting her straight, and occasionally that meant disciplining her, which bothered him.

She rolled her eyes. "Don't they say a little dirt don't hurt?"

"The farmers shoot all sorts of pesticides on them while they're growing." He tapped the fruit bowl. "Now you're eating those chemicals."

"Well, the good news is," she said around another bite of apple, "I'm apparently not a bug and will live." When she was finished, she acted as if she was making a three-point shot and tossed the core into the trash can. "What doesn't kill you makes you stronger and all that nonsense."

Evan flipped a dish towel over his shoulder as he loaded the dishwasher. "Did you come down here only to speak in platitudes or was there another reason you listened in on my conversation?"

"Ev, man, you're on point tonight." Laura hopped down from the counter. "Does she do this to you? That Claire?"

He almost asked what it meant to be "on point" but thought better of it. He'd never be able to keep up with his sister's ever-changing teenspeak.

"Claire—" Evan shut the dishwasher and jammed the Pots and Pans button to On "—does nothing to me. We're running against each other for mayor."

"I'm not stupid or a kid anymore. I know who Claire Atwood is."

"Of course you know who Claire Atwood is. Her dad is the biggest thing to happen to Goose Harbor since Goose Harbor became Goose Harbor."

Laura put her hands over her ears and squinted as if she was in pain. "Please don't say our town's name again for at least a week."

"Everyone knows who Claire is. She's royalty here."

"Royalty? Yeah, no. What I meant was, I know about you two." She offered him an exaggerated wink, as if they were in cahoots.

Evan tugged the dish towel off his shoulder and dropped it on the counter. "Joke's on you, because there's nothing to know."

"Huh." Laura grabbed the towel and hung it on the oven handle. "Except for the fact that you two were engaged."

"Secretly engaged—something I'm pretty sure I told you, so don't act like you have insider info." He tweaked her nose as he headed toward his office. Laura trailed after him, so he kept talking. "We were teens. We were stupid. It was a long time ago." He opened the French doors that led to his office and flipped on the overhead light. "It didn't go beyond that."

Laura beat him to the leather swivel chair behind his desk. She lifted her feet off the ground and tipped her head back, letting the chair whirl in a lazy circle. "Brice says she's the reason you don't date."

Evan focused on the framed art hung behind his desk. To the unsuspecting eye it was a simple painting of Lake Michigan and the dunes that hedged in Goose Harbor. But to him? The painting tugged at the part of his heart that still ached, still wished, still wanted more. Claire had given him the piece as a graduation present. Despite the beauty she'd captured with every stroke of her brush, she had always doubted her talent. Did she still paint?

It didn't matter.

Maybe he'd sell the painting.

He focused on Laura. "I'll have to have a talk with Brice then. He should keep his thoughts to himself instead of saying something like that to our kid sister."

Laura planted her feet to stop spinning. "He didn't say it to me. He said it to Kendall and I overheard."

Even worse. Kendall and Claire were friends. Hopefully, his almost-sister-in-law would keep something like that to herself. Then again, Kendall sometimes lacked a filter. He didn't want Claire to think he'd spent his life pining after her for all these years. A year or two, maybe, but he'd moved on. He simply didn't have the need or want for a woman in his life. He had enough on his plate between his business, his commitments at church and taking care of his sister.

Evan crossed his arms. "Overhearing seems to be a habit of yours."

"Not a habit, a talent." Laura waggled her eyebrows.

"A dangerous one at that." He came to her side of the desk and tapped on the back of the chair, signaling for her to get out of it. "'Oh be careful little ears what you hear.'" He hummed the rest of the little-kid song. They sometimes sung it with the younger children at Sunday school.

"Don't worry. It's not like I have anyone to tell," she grumbled as she got out of the chair then turned and tapped his chest. "And no offense, bro, but you're really not that exciting." Laura rose on her tiptoes and gave him a peck on the cheek. "But I love you, anyway."

Evan snagged her around her middle before she could get away, pulling her into a hug. "I love you, too. To Pluto and back."

She laughed against his chest. "Poor Pluto. He just wants to be a planet."

"Is he not anymore?" Evan set her back a bit but kept a hand on her shoulder. "I thought that had been reinstated?"

"Crazy galactic politics. Who can keep up?" She shrugged and stepped away.

He opened his laptop and finally took a seat at his desk. Laura made it to the doorway, but stopped and braced her hands on either side with her back to him.

"Did you need something?" Evan asked.

His sister twisted her head to look back at him. "She's really pretty."

"Claire's gorgeous." Evan glanced away. "She always was." And the label went far beyond the physical.

"Will you two ever be friends again?"

He sighed and shook his head. "Not likely." Evan clicked open a browser window. Might as well research what organizing a campaign entailed. "We're running against each other for the same position. That doesn't translate well into *let's be friends*."

"I guess." Laura started to leave, but then hooked her hand on the door frame and peeked her head in again. "Hey, do you think I can borrow twenty dollars? If you let me, I'll totally vote for you."

He laughed. So *that's* what she wanted all along. Evan fished his wallet from his back pocket and plucked out a twenty. "I won't even make you repay me."

Chapter Four

As a group of people brushed past her, Claire sent a text to her mother, reminding her that Alex should be in bed by eight because it was a school night. Tucking away her phone, she swept into the cavernous room inside town hall where the board meetings were held.

Large tubes along the ceiling attempted to pump heat into the area, but the system was so outdated it hardly worked anymore. Most of the residents seated in the rows of folding chairs that lined the room still had their coats and gloves on as if they were some grand penguin research committee preparing to meet at the South Pole. They angled their heads, catching up with neighbors that they hadn't seen in a week or two. During the other seasons, many of the Goose Harbor lifers spent time outside and walked or biked to run errands in the downtown square. They bumped into each other in the school pickup line and at the weekly farmers' market. But winter kept most people indoors, and with the lackluster tourist season, residents had gone longer than normal without a reason to come outside.

Perhaps Evan was right about the need to make good on the silly mayoral competition tradition. A morale boost could help everyone, and if Claire was the one smiling most brightly at the events, they'd look to her.

She spotted her cousin Jason, who was also the head reporter and editor for the town paper. He tipped the newsboy-style hat he was wearing toward her briefly and then turned away. Right, in public it was important to treat him as Jason Moss, the reporter...not Jay, her cousin. While people in town knew in theory that they were related, it was knowledge that was forgotten or not thought about when the papers came out, and that was best for Jason and his career. Once people put two and two together—that Claire's dad owned the paper that always printed nice pieces about him—Jason was the one who caught heat for it.

Claire lifted her chin, unhooked the first two buttons on her coat and strolled down the center aisle toward the front row, where she was supposed to sit for the specially called meeting. She stopped and spoke to a handful of people who sat on the outside of their rows.

A woman with spiked hair gave her hand a quick pump. "I heard you're running. I hope you do well."

"Thank you." Claire thought the woman was one of the teachers at the high school. She'd seen her before at functions held by Paige and Caleb Beck, who were both teachers, as well. The name Bree came to mind, but Claire wasn't confident enough about it being correct, so she offered an encouraging smile instead.

Claire grabbed a seat in the front row next to Shelby Beck, Caleb's sister. Shelby was curled up next to Joel Palermo, her fireman boyfriend—no, the sparkling diamond on Shelby's ring finger said Joel was now her fiancé.

Claire had to get better at talking to people, especially if she wanted to become the mayor. No time like the present.

"Congratulations." She leaned so her shoulder bumped Shelby's, and gestured toward the stunning princess-cut diamond. "I hadn't heard the news yet."

Shelby beamed. "Thank you! It only happened last weekend. And it was so perfect and romantic, I've been spending my time basking in it all."

"I'm happy for you," Claire offered. She didn't know Shelby or Joel well, but they'd already been a steady couple in town when Claire had returned, over a year ago. Both of them seemed like kind people. Joel had pulled over and changed Claire's tire during a rainstorm last fall when she'd gotten a flat. She'd told him she'd already placed a call to a car service, but he'd waved her off, told her to cancel the call and had gotten down on the wet pavement to work on her car. Joel had done that for her without being her friend, and he'd refused any form of payment.

"I've never been so happy in my life." Shelby squeezed Joel's arm to get his attention. He was in the middle of an exchange with one of his firefighter buddies, but he pivoted a little to catch Shelby's eye in case she needed him. Claire waved her hand, letting Shelby know not to bug him on her account.

The gavel came down on the podium, causing everyone to jump. Claire swiveled to face the front and her chest tightened when she discovered Evan Daniels sitting on her other side. "When did you—"

He put his finger to his lips. "Meeting's

been called to order," he whispered. "Banks takes these things way too seriously and—"

"Mr. Daniels." Mr. Banks laid down the gavel and peered over the podium. "The meeting has begun, and unless you can recite the entire agenda already, I will ask you to remain quiet so everyone can enjoy the proceedings."

Evan raised a hand and turned toward the crowd. "My apologies." He flashed an "I'm going to Disneyland!" smile, which was met with a smattering of light chuckles by residents who clearly adored him.

Mr. Banks tugged his pants up past his belly button as he scowled at Evan. "If you're done with your little show, I'd like to continue."

Evan bowed his head and stretched his hand out like a waiter. "By all means." Ever so slightly he leaned toward Claire and murmured. "Just me, or was that a flashback to second period Spanish?"

Claire stifled a laugh, which made Mr. Banks glower in her direction. She sank lower in her chair. "Not just you."

Evan had been terrible at picking up languages and Claire hadn't been much better. Their struggle with the class might have had more to do with the fact that they spent the bulk of the time passing notes back and forth instead of listening. Señora Ojeda used to stop the class to tsk at them regularly.

Mr. Banks cleared his throat. "Many of you know that I will be stepping down from the position of interim mayor next month."

"Not soon enough!" someone in the back shouted.

Banks worked his jaw back and forth.

Claire glanced at Evan. "Is it always like this?"

He grinned, nodded. "We should have brought popcorn."

Banks pushed away from the podium. "The board and I have been discussing the merits required for the position. I'm sure many of you are asking yourselves, what makes an excellent mayor?"

"The last name Ashby doesn't hurt," someone called from the crowd. That was met with a round of agreements.

"Best mayor we ever had."

"Is the new Ashby running?"

"I sure miss Ida."

"Tough crowd," Evan mumbled.

Kellen Ashby, nephew of the longest-serving mayor, raised his hands in a way that said *it wasn't me* as all heads turned in his direction. "I promise I didn't pay anyone to shout that."

His oldest daughter bounced in her seat. "Dad, you *should* be mayor! Everyone vote for my dad!"

"Skylar." Kellen settled a hand on her knee. "The man's trying to lead a meeting."

Skylar shook her head and said even louder, "He used to be a rock star. You should totally vote for him." Ruthy, Kellen's youngest daughter, grinned from ear to ear as she nodded along with her sister.

Maggie, Kellen's wife, wrapped her arm around the noisy offender and said, "Hush!" The family of four was all smiles. "I'm so sorry." Maggie gave a small wave. "Please keep going."

Mr. Banks shuffled his notes. "Don't even know why I try." He harrumphed and adjusted his glasses. "Here we are." He held one of his sheets of paper out as far as his arm would go. "After a *lengthy* meeting the board has decided that our ideal mayoral candidate must excel at problem solving and creativity, must be poised and well-spoken, and must be able to work with others in an organized yet detailed manner."

His giant eyebrows looked like two angry caterpillars glued to his forehead. He lowered them and scanned the room, a silent challenge to anyone who would make another smart-aleck comment. "Problem solving is essential to the task of mayor, especially when it comes to juggling our need for tourism with the equally important needs of our year-round residents. Often the two are in opposition, so creativity comes in handy when coupled with problem solving."

"Right. How much creativity do you think Banks has ever used?" One of the firemen in the second row made the comment a little too loudly to a buddy nearby.

Banks frowned. "Believe me, I am using every ounce of creativity I possess right this very minute. A thank-you is due to you, Lieutenant Marcus of our esteemed Goose Harbor Fire Department, for demonstrating exactly *why* a poised and a well-spoken person is necessary in this position." He smacked his note-cards against the podium. "I'm certain your chief is very proud."

The fireman looked down and studied his hands, embarrassed at being publicly called out.

"And since this town is not a dictatorship—although, believe me, that *would* make things easier—the ability to work on a team with people you probably don't like is paramount as well."

Mr. Banks looked suddenly very tired and old, and Claire felt sorry for him. He hadn't asked to be put in the position he was in. He'd stepped up because the last mayor had left without much warning. Banks was doing the best he could. So what if he was a bit—okay, a lot—of a curmudgeon? If Claire won it would be her up there dealing with the boisterous and jovial crowd.

Would she be able to handle all the interruptions with as much finesse as he had? She smoothed her hair behind her ears and ducked her head, studying the worn patterns on the floor.

Did she even want to deal with all this?

After Mr. Banks announced Evan and Claire as formal candidates, he explained the competitions that would take place, and finally adjourned the meeting.

Evan made his way to the double doors so he could greet and visit with people as they filed out.

Kellen Ashby passed by. He held Ruthy, his youngest daughter, in one arm and had his other around his wife's shoulders. Evan and he exchanged a chin-up form of greeting.

Skylar, skipping behind, dodged around him. "Sorry, Mr. Evan. I can't shake your hand, seeing how I'm not going to vote for you."

Evan braced his hands on his thighs to come down to her level. "Well, that's sad."

Maggie snagged her arm. "Come on, sweetheart. Leave poor Evan alone."

Skylar took Maggie's hand, but called over her shoulder, "If I could vote, I'd have to vote for my dad."

Evan saluted her. "If your dad was running, I might vote for him, too."

For a few minutes the din of conversation near the front doors was so loud Evan had to lean close and raise his voice in order to converse with his neighbors. Almost everyone stopped to wish him well.

"I'm supposed to be impartial, of course." Mrs. Clarkson cupped her hands around Evan's. She leaned into his personal space, bringing the heavy smells of coffee and baby powder with her. "With me working part-time at the town hall office, you know how that can be. They want me to be some opinionless robot about these matters. As if anyone could really, deep down, be that way." She looked from side to side, like a secret agent relaying vital information. "Now this is strictly between me and you, but I sure do hope you win, son."

"Your secret is safe with me." Evan winked.

Mrs. Clarkson swatted him in the shoulder, and then zipped her coat and squared her shoulders as she headed into the cold with the rest of the dwindling crowd.

Claire filled the other side of the double doors. She had talked to people who exited that way, but now that they were mostly gone, she and Evan were only a few feet apart, staring at each other.

She crossed her arms and raised her eyebrows. "Well, that was quick."

"What?" he asked.

"You said you weren't going to flirt to win."

"You think?" Evan's jaw went slack. "With *Mrs. Clarkson*?" He pointed at the door. Claire *had* to be kidding. Did she really think so little of him to imagine he'd toy with an elderly woman's emotions like that? She'd been somewhat of a mother-figure in his life. "That was not flirting."

"It was."

"No. Absolutely not." Evan shook his head and stepped forward. Letting the door close behind him, he moved into the entryway where Claire waited. "Flirting carries intent.

I have no intent there besides being kind to a nice old lady."

"I don't agree with you."

"Which is your right. Free country and all." He made his way to the rack where his coat was hanging and pulled it off the hanger. "You can believe whatever you want to, but doing so doesn't make it true." He tugged on his coat and jammed his hands into the pockets.

"I'm fairly certain the textbook definition of flirting says something about not having serious intent."

"I don't care about textbooks, Claire. You know what I mean."

"Evan. Relax." Claire's laugh was light, almost like the old days. She slipped on her coat and tugged a hat out of her pocket. "I'm teasing you." She set the hat on her head. "Although it's not as much fun when I have to explain it."

A few days ago they weren't speaking to each other. Now they were back to teasing? When he'd snagged the seat beside her at the start of the meeting Evan hadn't known what to expect. Would she be upset or angry that he'd settled next to her? But she hadn't been either. They'd shared a few laughs. She'd seemed to enjoy his company. He didn't know what to do with it all. Shouldn't he say something?

Claire's quick comebacks had always been able to turn his brain to mush.

The front door banged open, revealing Jason Moss, the editor of the local newspaper. He had a huge camera slung around his neck. "I just got off the phone. Had to go outside to hear over the crowd in here." He jiggled his cell in his hand. "My normal photographer is out sick this evening, so unfortunately, you guys are stuck with me."

Evan looked at Claire to see if she knew what Jason was talking about, but confusion colored her features.

"Sorry, Jay," she said. Her gaze volleyed between Jason and Evan. "We don't know what you're talking about."

"I need to do a photo shoot with the two of you." Jason jiggled the camera. "Nothing fancy. We'll just snap a couple and I'll run the best one with the article I'm doing for the election. The newspaper one will be printed in black-and-white, but we'll need a couple decent ones for the website and our social media pages."

She adjusted her hat. "Right now?"

Jason rammed his hip into the metal bar on the door, holding it open for them. A cold blast of winter sliced through the lobby. "It would be best to get it done while we still have a half hour or so of sunlight left."

Evan ushered Claire out the door, letting her go first, and they followed Jason down the slick path toward the street. Claire picked her way carefully over the shoveled walkway. Her heels were lower than she normally wore, but they probably didn't afford her much traction. Evan made a point to stay near enough to grab her elbow, to steady her if she slipped.

Jason stopped abruptly. He turned in a circle, scrutinizing the area. "I thought we could do a few here in front of town hall and then move to the town square. Take one or two on a bench there, and possibly at the gazebo."

Snow crunched under Evan's boots. "Sounds fine to me."

Jason motioned for them to stand together between the flags hanging on either side of the front doors. "Smile." He held up the camera. "Stand closer. I know you two are running against each other, but this isn't the White House here. We're a friendly place. We want friendly looking pictures on our website. Act like you like each other a little."

"Here." Claire took Evan by the shoulders. "Stand there. Let's do backs together." She leaned against his back and they both crossed their arms and smiled for the camera.

Jason snapped a few and then started toward the center of town. "If we still have some light after the gazebo, I'd like to hike over to the swing set near the grade school just off the square."

"The swing set?" Claire balked.

"You two went to school together, am I right?"

"Well, yes, but…" Claire looked to Evan, but he only shrugged. She and Jason were related; he wasn't about to get in the middle if this turned into an argument.

Jason moved his hand as if he was running it over the top of a table. "Everyone here knows that. So let's capitalize on it."

He snapped a few shots of them on the bench and a few more on the steps of the gazebo. As they tromped toward the school yard, Claire lobbed a snowball that struck Evan's shoulder, taking him by surprise. She'd been quiet during most of the photos.

"This isn't a war you want to start," Evan warned her.

"Please." She held her hands up in surrender. "Jason made me. He wanted it for a picture."

"A picture, huh? What about this one?"

Evan scooped up a handful of snow, packed it and tossed it at Claire. She screamed and started running toward the swing set. Evan chased after her. When they reached the swings Jason was far behind them and they were both heaving to catch their breath.

"Man." Evan held his side. "I'm out of shape."

"Hardly." Claire dusted off one of the swings, sat down and started pumping her legs. "You might be in even better shape than you were at eighteen." Her gaze swept over him from head to toe before she looked away, toward the horizon. From the top of the swing's arc, the lake was visible.

"I'll say this much." Evan snagged the remaining swing and joined her. "My eighteen-year-old lungs wouldn't be burning right now."

Jason snapped a few pictures while they swung. "Okay, that's enough. I'm freezing and I'm sure I got something usable. We're done here." He headed back in the direction of the square, leaving Evan and Claire behind on the swings as the sun's light drained from the sky. They were silent for a while, long enough for Jason's car to disappear. Evan stopped moving his legs, allowing himself to coast to a stop, but Claire kept going.

In a lot of ways it was a true picture of her. She had always been driven to be the best, to prove that she was top dog. She'd achieved the highest scores in school. Evan had always figured it was an attempt to impress Sesser, and maybe that's exactly what it was. But maybe not. She and Evan might have kissed in the park after school, but he'd never asked Claire what drove her. Never got to the bottom of what made Claire Atwood tick.

Evan dug his boots into the snow until his ankles grew cold.

Examining it all now, he'd been a terrible boyfriend to Claire. He'd thought he loved her, thought he'd showed her love and treated her well. But he'd been a foolish boy from a messed up family and knew nothing about what loving someone looked like.

He was still that foolish boy. At least now he understood his complete inadequacy when it came to functional relationships. He wouldn't burden another woman with his ineptitude again like he had Claire. She deserved a guy who understood how to love her, and never messed up.

Claire reached the top of the arc and jumped off the swing. She landed on her feet and bowed for an imaginary crowd before

turning in his direction with her fist raised
high. "I've still got it!"

The streetlamps clicked on, along with the
white Christmas lights that still hung in in-
tricate webs in the trees around the square.
The soft glow illuminated Claire, making her
red hair glow and lighting up her face enough
to show her flushed cheeks. Evan's breath
hitched. He'd never seen anyone more beautiful than Claire in that moment.

He got to his feet and slowly clapped for
her. "Quite a feat, for us old folks."

One of her eyes squinted and she puckered
her lips as she studied him. "I'll take that as
a compliment, because I'm feeling gracious."

Evan made his way through the snow to
her, his toes numb. "A good trait for a mayoral candidate."

"Though it wasn't on 'the list.'" She put air
quotes around the last two words.

Evan came alongside her. "Can I walk you
back to your car?" He offered his arm. "The
sidewalk's slick. You're wearing heels and—"

"And I've been known to take a spill occasionally. Yes. I remember."

"Although, your run through the snow on
the way to the swings was impressive, so
maybe you're fine without me," he joked.

"That was through the snow and now we're

on the iced sidewalk." She grimaced and then took his arm. "I'll accept your assistance."

Snow compressed beneath their steps. Branches on a nearby tree popped and stiff wind directly off Lake Michigan pushed through the square. Some of the powdery flakes that had fallen earlier lifted back into the air for one last dance.

"Claire." He steered them onto the brick street. "I know you don't want to talk about the past."

"Please, Evan, don't."

"I won't." They slowed as they entered the archway of lit trees. "Not about…that."

"Thank you," she said, so softly he almost didn't hear.

Evan glanced up through the branches wrapped with lights and focused at the stars scattered across the night sky. "But I did want to say that I wish I had been a better friend to you, back then." He chanced a look her way. "A true, good friend, like you needed. I wasn't. I'm sorry about that."

She unwound her arm from his. "It was a long time ago."

"I'm still sorry." He stopped. They were less than ten feet from her car.

"Well, thank you. I think." She searched for her keys in her purse. When she found them, she clicked the button that made her car chirp. "I'd like it if we could at least be civil to each other from now on. Especially since they're making us work on a service project together for our teamwork challenge."

"Not only work together," Evan corrected her in a good-natured way. "Completely plan and execute a fund-raiser." He ran his hand over his hair. "That's going to be a handful."

Claire opened her car and then turned back to him. She hooked her hand on top of the open door. "It may be asking a lot, but when we're planning that can we either do it at your house or in a neutral location?"

"Your dad still doesn't want me on his property, huh?"

"You're not his favorite person."

"Still?"

"I think forever."

"Gotcha." He stuck his hands in the deep pockets of his coat. He really needed to start remembering to bring gloves. "You and Alex are welcome at my house anytime."

Claire left in her car, but Evan stayed and strolled through the square for a few minutes. He had wanted to say something more, to offer to be her friend now, but how could he? They were running against each other. In the coming weeks, they would have to do a round of competitions. When all was said and done, one would beat the other, and he could hardly imagine maintaining a friendship after that.

Chapter Five

Claire breezed into Fair Tradewinds Coffee, a mom-and-pop shop along the pier in Goose Harbor that served some of the best coffee she had ever tasted. And the inside decor always made her smile, because they took the nautical theme to the extreme. The baristas dressed like sailors. A large sign hanging near the register proclaimed Every Boat Is a Good Boat!

"Ahoy! What can we get you?" A barista held a cup and a marker in her hands, poised to jot down Claire's order. Did the employees ever get sick of the mishmash of pirate-and-sailorspeak they were supposed to sprinkle into their conversations?

Kendall's arm shot up from where she sat at one of the back tables. Claire let her know she saw her and then turned to order. It was early and she had a long day ahead of her, so she should probably caffeinate, but all she wanted was hot chocolate.

"This might be a strange request," she said to the cashier. "But can I get peanut butter in my hot chocolate? If you have any?"

The woman punched at buttons on her machine and then pushed her glasses up her nose. "Aye, we can. As long as chocolate peanut butter cups will do. Mr. Daniels takes his that way, so we keep them on hand."

"That would be lovely." Claire paid and waited for her order at the second counter. Would the barista tell Evan that Claire had used some of his reserve peanut butter cups? Not that it mattered. She was allowed to take her drink however she wanted it. It wasn't just because of him that she wanted hot chocolate made a certain way. When they called her name she snagged her drink and then made her way to Kendall.

Kendall's gigantic mug was almost empty. She eyed Claire's cup. "Don't tell me you got the Screaming Joe."

The owner of Fair Tradewinds Coffee was known for making strange drink concoctions and tricking tourists into buying them. The shop was famous for the Screaming Joe, a cup supposedly filled with equal portions of coffee and hot sauce…and who knew what else. Throughout the summer younger tourists could be seen attempting to down a cup of it with tears streaming down their faces. Somehow, they all still came, drank and uploaded photos of each other chugging the horrible mix. It had become a can't-miss stop for many visitors.

Claire grinned. "Afraid not. Just hot cocoa."

"Not coffee. Who is this new Claire? I don't even know you!" Kendall tugged out the chair closest to her and patted the seat. "I feel like we haven't gotten to catch up in ages."

"That's because you're busy planning your wedding!" Claire lowered her bag and mug onto the table and gave Kendall a quick side hug. "And soon you'll be all married and I won't be able to catch up with you at all."

"No way." Kendall pulled a face. "Marriage isn't going to change that. You know how much Brice needs his alone time! I'll leave him at home to introvert while you and me paint the town."

Claire stirred her hot cocoa, helping the peanut butter cup melt. "I still can't believe Brice is completely fine with us being friends."

Kendall pushed her empty mug to the center of the table and gave Claire a thoughtful look. "Brice is my soon-to-be husband, not my boss. He doesn't decide who is my friend and who isn't." She eased her elbows onto the table and sank her chin into her hands. "I mean, yes, I ask and want his advice. But he knows how much I care about you and that you're my best and, seriously, my first real gal pal." She let one of her hands drop to cover Claire's. "He's just happy for me. That's what he really wants. Me to be happy."

Claire slipped her hand free and picked up her cup. "Sounds nice."

Kendall's brow furrowed. "Do I hear skepticism?"

"No skepticism here. I promise." She took a sip, but it was still too hot, so she set down her cup. "Okay, I guess it just seems too good to be true." She shrugged out of her coat and hung it over the back of her chair. "I've watched my parents. My dad tells me and my mom who we can and can't talk to, be friends with, associate with. He has always had total say. It's hard to believe it's not like that in all relationships." Claire lowered her voice as she spoke, knowing that if her father found out she'd said such things he'd have plenty of words for her.

Thankfully, the coffee shop was crowded and loud, and they would be hard to overhear.

"Claire, you're a grown woman. You don't have to do what he says anymore."

"Sure." Claire gave a humorless laugh that held a bitter edge. "I'm a grown woman who got a lot of advanced degrees on my dad's dime. Then I failed at doing the one thing that would have made both my parents happy."

Kendall pursed her lips, considering her for a heartbeat before speaking again. "Do you mean backing out of things with Auden?"

Kendall was the only one who knew the entire backstory of Auden Pierce, and why Claire had ended things with him. Her friend had been supportive and encouraging, and Claire appreciated that, but she really hoped Kendall hadn't told Brice or Evan all the things she'd trusted her with. Could she really trust anyone? Claire's gut told her no—people were always looking for a way to one-up each other, or use information for personal gain. But so far, Kendall had done nothing to warrant such doubt.

Claire watched the steam from her cocoa leech into the air. "I don't know if it was my mom or dad who was more disappointed. All my dad has ever asked of me was to marry a guy who could be trusted to run his business someday. Auden could have done that." Claire ended with a shrug.

"But you didn't love him."

"Who knows? When it comes to love—at least romantic love—I don't think I'd know it even if it was staring me in the eye. I thought I knew…but it burned me in the past." She laced her fingers around her cup and took a long drink, avoiding Kendall's searching gaze.

That wasn't right either, though, because Evan hadn't loved her. He couldn't have. If Claire understood anything about love she at least knew that it didn't abandon people.

However, Claire *had* loved Evan completely. She'd loved him so much her heart had ached for years after they'd split. Like a lovesick puppy, she'd written to him during her freshman year of college, begging for an explanation. Evan had never written back.

That was not love.

She would never lose herself to that feeling again, fall so hard that she was blinded to the truth—that a guy would never love her like she'd once thought Evan had. Not while she carried the name Atwood like a heavy weight around her neck. Her father's influence was a part of every relationship in her life, even her friendship with Kendall. They were friends because Claire had originally served as the go-between when Kendall and her father had been silent business partners.

Claire needed to say something before Kendall started asking probing questions, as she was known to do.

"Auden is a lot like my father. He was always busy and only there for me when it was convenient or beneficial to him. We probably would have had a fine marriage. He was respectful enough."

"Respectful *enough*? Claire, do you even hear yourself?"

She shrugged. "Sometimes I think I should have gone through with the wedding. If we were married now, my parents would be thrilled."

An image came to mind. *Alex*. She'd dropped him off for a playdate at the Holcombs' apple orchard on her way to coffee. Auden had made it clear that he wanted only biological children. She'd started the adoption paperwork behind his back in a moment when she was doubting their relationship. She'd always had a desire to adopt children, and Auden constantly shut her down whenever the topic came up. That's what had given her the courage to break off their engagement in the end.

"Look at me." Kendall snapped her fingers.

"You did the right thing. Hear that. Take that in—don't question it. And do you want to hear something else?"

Claire placed her now empty cup beside Kendall's. "I'm sure you're going to tell me whether I say yes or no, so go ahead."

"You love me *because* I say whatever I want."

"You're right."

Kendall reached over and gathered both Claire's hands into her own. She squeezed them until Claire met her eyes. "Right here, right now, I'm freeing you from the need to please your parents."

"What?" Claire tried to pull her hands away, but Kendall held firm.

"As of this day, you no longer are responsible for your parents' happiness. The only ones you should be worried about pleasing are God and yourself. That's it. End of list."

Kendall finally let go. Claire wove her fingers together in her lap and looked down at them. "Easy for you to say."

"Wrong. That's actually superdifficult for me to say." Kendall tapped the table. "Until last year, I believed my father had walked out on me because he didn't want me. For years, so many years, I tried to prove that I was worth loving, and you know what? God loved me that whole time. I didn't have anything to prove. It was all useless striving."

She made a grand sweeping motion with her hand. "I'm free of that now and it feels so...so good to know I'm loved for me—by God, by Brice, by you." She pressed her fingertips over her heart. "And you know my life isn't perfect. My mom is gone, Claire. I may never see her again. She can't accept that I'm a Christian now or that I've put boundaries on my life that she doesn't agree with. If I focus on all that it upsets me, but I can't live to please her, either."

Claire knew Kendall's story and found encouragement in it, but they were different scenarios. "I still live with my parents. It makes it all very tricky."

"That is a tightrope to walk, I'll give you that." Kendall waggled her finger. "Can I ask about your run for mayor? Is that your doing or your dad's?"

"He was just as surprised as everyone else. Of course, he's happy now that he thinks I might become the mayor, because he's imagining all the ways it could benefit him. But I chose to run." Claire traced a coffee ring on the table. "I wanted... I know it sounds childish, but for once I wanted to matter to this town beyond my connection to the name Atwood. Does that make sense?"

"It does." Kendall nodded enthusiastically. "And I support you in making decisions like this on your own. I want you to keep on this track."

"But I don't have your vote?" Claire gave her friend a wry smile, letting her know she was kidding.

Kendall grinned back. "You *are* running against my sweet soon-to-be brother-in-law. He loves this place, too."

"I know he does."

"Speaking of, Brice talked to Evan the other night and he said something about the board running you guys through a battery of tests. Did I hear that right?" Kendall rose to her feet and Claire did likewise. They both gathered their belongings and headed outside. Kendall had a meeting with the chef who would be catering her wedding that she had to get to.

Light snow cascaded across the lake, fat, puffy snowflakes. The kind that made Claire want to try to catch one on her tongue…if she wasn't in the middle of downtown, where anyone could see her. Maybe she'd convince Alex to go play outside with her later. She needed to practice for tomorrow's first event and that could be her excuse.

"It's an old tradition that the town hasn't needed to make good on until now," Claire explained. "We have to engage in friendly competitions that prove we are well-spoken and have problem-solving skills, creativity and the ability to work on a team." She had parked next to Kendall's car, so they headed toward the parking lot side by side. "For problem solving the math teachers from the high school are putting together an exam for us to take, and tomorrow Evan and I have to build snow sculptures in the square to demonstrate how creative we are."

"You've got to be kidding me." Kendall laughed so hard she snorted. "Goose Harbor is the best place ever."

"It's definitely unique." Claire clicked the button on her key fob to unlock the doors. "For the teamwork challenge Evan and I have to plan a fund-raiser together to host on the Saturday of Valentine's weekend."

Kendall grabbed her arm and her eyes went wide. "That's less than two weeks away! I plan events for a living and even I think that's madness."

"Tell that to Mr. Banks."

"No way!" She gave an exaggerated shiver.

"I'm terrified of him. What about the last one? How do you prove you're well-spoken?"

"That one's easy, at least. We'll both have the floor in a town hall meeting before voting opens on the day of the election. I'm not worried about that part."

No, it was only 100 percent of the rest of the challenges that had Claire second-guessing her decision. And not for the first time, either.

Someone was pounding on Evan's front door.

He considered going upstairs to put his contacts in, but decided against it. His eyesight wasn't terrible. He ran a cloth over his countertop, because it looked like Laura had engaged in a late night snack and had left the crumbs as evidence. Then he tossed the rag into the sink and jogged to answer the door. The second he flipped the lock the door swung open. He had to jump to the side to get out of the way.

Brice tossed a newspaper at him. "Have you seen this?"

Evan scrambled to catch the paper and fumbled a couple times. When he finally had it, he jammed the newsprint under his arm and squinted at his brother. "Good morning?"

Brice rarely showed up at his house unannounced...rarely ventured to his house at all. For him to come over something must be—

Evan froze. "Please tell me Mom and Dad are all right." It was an irrational question, but so many of their adult years had revolved around putting out fires for their parents that it came out automatically.

Brice frowned. "You think they would call me before you? Not likely. You're the golden child. They both hate me."

An apology crawled its way up Evan's throat for the thousandth time, but he swallowed it. How did a man go about telling his brother he was sorry that their mother doted on one son, while she was cruel and hurtful to the other? Brice didn't like to discuss their childhood, how he'd taken punch after punch from their father, while Evan had left the house basically unscathed. Evan owed Brice everything.

His brother climbed onto one of the bar stools. "Have you heard from either of them lately?"

"Dad's been gone for a couple weeks." Evan padded over to the kitchen island and laid the newspaper on the counter. "Mom's not sure where he's at this time. She's okay. The same. The house is a wreck but you know that. I told her I'd hire a company to come clear it out, but she wouldn't hear of it."

"Sounds about right." Brice pointed up to indicate the second story of the house. "How's Laura?"

Evan scrubbed his hand over his face. "Sleeping. They practice late for the musical."

His brother propped his hands together and pressed the sides of his pointer fingers to his lips. "Are you sure she's not just telling you it lets out late?"

"She's not lying to me."

It was for the best that Laura had moved in with Evan. Brice meant well, but he was too overbearing sometimes, especially when it came to their youngest sibling. Evan got the feeling that Brice believed he had failed their brother Andrew, so he had to make up for it by not failing their sister. Whenever the topic of Andrew's disappearance came up, Brice harped on the fact that he should have, could have, done more to be there for him. He'd become even more protective of Laura once Andrew left.

Brice arched an eyebrow. "She's seventeen and I know she's got more than one guy after her."

"Have a little faith in her. She's a good kid."

"When you were seventeen—" Brice tapped

the stone countertop "—you and Claire were off sneaking around together. If—"

"Then let's be thankful that our sister is a better person than I was at that age," Evan interrupted. It wasn't often that they disagreed, or that he pushed back on anything Brice wanted, but for their sister he would. "Laura's not me, so let's not make wild assumptions based on my mistakes."

Brice straightened in the chair. Rolled his shoulders. Were they going to argue?

But then— "You'll make a good father someday."

Evan ran his tongue over the back of his teeth; his mouth tasted sour. "I'm not interested in being a dad."

"Yes you are."

He was, but being a dad meant having a woman in his life, and he'd long ago come to the conclusion that he couldn't live up to what a woman needed in a man. What kind of guy let his own brother take beatings for him? Or left the person he loved because of blackmail? Every time he thought about it Evan was left feeling…less. Less than Brice. Less than a man.

His eyes burned. He had to stop thinking about that part of his life. He had a good business; he enjoyed his neighbors and had an excellent relationship with most of his siblings. Wanting more out of life was greedy and wrong.

"Not that I don't enjoy your company, but why'd you stop by?"

"The front page. Give it a look." Brice yanked off his baseball hat and wound it around in his hands.

Evan yawned. "I woke up all of about ten minutes ago, so give a guy a second."

Brice jabbed his finger at the picture on the front page. "Did you know they were going to run an article like this?"

His eyes finally came into focus. The front page had a large picture of him and Claire on the steps of the town hall building. It was one of the first shots Jason had taken—of them standing back-to-back. Another smaller picture showed the two of them on the swings.

Evan grabbed a box of cereal from the top of his fridge and started eating a handful.

Brice shook his head, clearly trying to hide the fact that he wanted to smile. "There's a cartoon character on your breakfast." He tapped the box.

"Yup." Evan tossed another handful of cereal into his mouth. "It has marshmallows, too. Want some?"

"I had eggs and bacon at home." Brice examined the side of the box where the nutritional information was printed. "You feed Laura this kind of stuff?"

"I give her money and send her to the grocery store and she comes back with this. It's wonderful."

"You're making me think that her moving here wasn't a good idea."

"Oh, stop being grumpy. When push comes to shove, you know I cook significantly better than you. At your house it's meat and nothing else. Here, I toss in the occasional seasoning." He held the paper close enough to get the print into focus and read the headline. "Ten Reasons to Vote for Claire Atwood."

Brice folded his hands together and nodded. "Interesting, wouldn't you say?"

Evan stopped reading. "Everyone knows Sesser owns the paper. No one takes it seriously."

Brice moved the paper so it was in front of him. He smoothed out the section Evan had wrinkled when he'd caught it earlier. "It details all of her achievements and degrees, while highlighting that you have none."

Evan opened the freezer and pulled out a carton of French vanilla ice cream. He fished a spoon from the silverware drawer, poured some cereal on top of the ice cream and took a bite.

Brice watched him. "You're eating pure sugar for breakfast."

"Exactly." He took another bite. Licked the spoon for effect. "It's the best time to eat it. Now I have the rest of the day to work it off." He tapped his stomach.

"You've got to be kidding me." Brice fake gagged. He was more of a meat-and-potatoes guy. Evan would be surprised if his brother ate cake at his own wedding.

"Laura forgot to buy milk." He shrugged. "But she picked up three tubs of ice cream on sale. Buy two, get one free. You can't pass up something like that."

Brice dropped his face into his hands. "How are we supposed to sell you as someone who can run this town if you can't even eat normal, healthy food?"

"Listen." Evan dropped the spoon into the sink with a loud clang and put the ice cream away. "It wasn't my idea to run for mayor. And I had grilled asparagus for dinner last night. It all balances out. Besides, I already knew about the pictures, and I figured Jason would write an article to go along with them."

"You did?"

"I was there when the photos were taken.

There are more on the town's website, I'm told. Jason wanted to use them to make Goose Harbor look appealing—and isn't that something a mayor should want?" He rinsed his hands off at the faucet and moved the spoon into the dishwasher. "If it makes you feel any better, I guess Sesser is livid about the pictures. Claire texted me this morning—"

"Hold up. You and she are texting each other?" Brice glared at the cell phone lying near the sink. "Since when?"

Evan scooped up the phone and stuck it in his pocket. "Since the board declared that we have to plan a fund-raiser together. Do you know how difficult that is to do on short notice? So yeah, we have to be in touch. It's fine."

Brice's brow scrunched with worry. "Are you sure you're okay with that?"

"Why wouldn't I be?"

"Evan." Brice slipped off the stool and latched on to his forearm as he tried to walk past. "You loved that woman."

"I loved her when we were teenagers." Evan snaked out of his brother's grasp and made a beeline for the couch. "That was a long time ago. We're both completely different people now." He flopped down so he was looking up at the ceiling. "I'm slightly more mature than I was back then, although I do still eat cartoon cereal for breakfast. Sometimes I even have pudding cups for a snack."

Brice bunched his hands into the fabric on the back of the couch. "I don't want to see you hurt again. After that all went down... you were devastated."

Evan slung his arm over his eyes, blocking his brother out. Brice didn't know the half of it. On the day he and Claire were going to elope, Sesser had cornered him and showed Evan how his father had taken out massive loans in Brice's name. More money than the Danielses could ever pay back. If Evan walked away from Claire, Sesser would make the debts disappear, but if he insisted on pursuing her, Sesser had threatened to use his vast influence to get Brice thrown out of the college he was attending. Not only that, but he'd promised to see that Brice would never receive admittance anywhere else. Evan hadn't doubted that the man had the power and connections to make good on his intimidations. And yet... Evan had hesitated until Sesser pledged to pay for all Brice's college tuition anonymously.

Of course, Brice knew none of that, and if it was up to Evan, he never would. Brice had sacrificed again and again to take care of and protect his siblings. The deal Evan had been forced into with Sesser was a drop in the bucket compared to what he owed his brother.

Evan lifted his arm. Brice was still there, watching, waiting, probably overanalyzing.

"I'll be fine."

After his brother left, Evan answered the latest text from Claire, letting her know Alex and she were welcome to stop by later to start working on their teamwork assignment. He added one last message, inviting them to dinner. Then he got up, snagged the newspaper off the counter and went and filed it in his desk. Claire looked so happy in the pictures, and he wanted to keep them for after the election when they wouldn't be forced to spend time together any longer. At least then he'd have the images of her smiling.

Chapter Six

Alex's teacher had caught Claire while she was shopping in the square earlier and detailed some issues he'd been having in class. He'd been struggling with focusing, he'd picked fights with other students and he'd argued with the teacher and broken down into full-out sobs a few times. The teacher believed Alex might be a better fit for a specialized class or school. Claire had volleyed between choices the rest of the day.

Attachment disorder.

That's what the doctor had scrawled in Alex's file after a series of psychological evaluations. He wasn't a typical kid acting out; this was the behavior of someone who was terrified to allow people near emotionally—especially people who actively tried to be a part of his life. Claire kept reminding herself of that. She reminded herself of the advice from the doctor every day: keep showing him love, stay steady, have a sense of humor and keep in mind he didn't hate her, he just didn't yet know what to do with someone saying they'd have his back for the long haul. The number one rule the doctor gave her? Don't take it personally.

It sure felt personal.

Eight months of tantrums—of holes kicked into the walls, of him shutting her out—had worn her thin. Sometimes he was well behaved, but even then didn't respond positively toward her. Strangers often had an easier time connecting with him, at least in short exchanges. Supposedly that was part of his diagnosis, too.

What had she really expected when she'd chosen to become an adoptive mother? Naively, she'd pictured her new son cuddling on her lap, asking to go for walks with her and instantly feeling like a family together.

So far, none of that had happened. On his birthday, he'd asked to be left alone.

Alex had been quiet on the drive to Evan's house, almost moody, and Claire worried that he might act out or say something outlandish when they arrived. Instead, he had rushed out of the car and hadn't stopped talking from the moment Evan answered the door.

They were setting the table as Claire threw together the ingredients she'd brought to make a salad, although she was pretty sure that the salad would go untouched next to the garlic French bread and asiago chicken drenched in bacon cream sauce that Evan had whipped up. His house smelled as good as her last trip to Italy.

"Did you know that there aren't any penguins in the northern hemisphere?" Alex trailed after Evan as he set plates on the table. "Christmas movies with penguins at the North Pole are wrong. They live at the South Pole."

Evan handed him a stack of napkins. "You just taught me something new. If I'm ever on a game show and win money for knowing that, I'll split my bounty with you."

"I know all about a lot of animals."

"You're my go-to guy when it comes to animal facts."

Alex puffed out his chest. Claire ceased mixing the salad and watched the two guys interacting. She wouldn't deny that Alex displayed more confidence around Evan. It was abnormal for him to be this talkative within minutes of entering a home he'd never been to before. But Evan had taken him under his wing and started joking with him before Alex even had his coat off.

"That caterpillar you told me about last Sunday at church?" Evan continued. "The one that lives in the Arctic and freezes solid for four months every year? It was genius."

"That's the banded woolly bear caterpillar."

Evan spun to bring Claire into the conversation. "Did he tell you about this thing?"

She carried her salad over to the table. "I have no clue what you guys are talking about."

"Get this." Evan rested a hand on Alex's shoulder. "This caterpillar lives for fourteen years before becoming a moth. Every winter they freeze solid—their heart stops."

Alex gripped the back of the chair and bounced on the balls of his feet. "They're very much dead."

Evan's dimples appeared as he watched Alex. "What science would consider dead, anyway."

"But the secret is, every spring they thaw and come back to life!" Alex tossed his hands in the air and did a slow, dramatic circle.

Claire clapped her hand over her mouth. She'd never seen Alex act this way—so free. She squeaked out, "That *is* amazing."

Evan motioned for everyone to take a seat. "Alex brought it up in Sunday school and Mr. Woolly, as we took to calling him, really helped demonstrate the point I was trying to make for the kids. The entire objective of a caterpillar's life is to become something more, something better, right?"

"A butterfly," Claire offered.

Alex dropped his chin into his hand and gave a frustrated sigh. "The woolly becomes a moth, Mom." His feet beat against the bar under his chair like a metronome.

"Sorry." Claire grimaced in apology for Alex's sake. "Moth."

Evan sent Alex a wink and then turned to address her. "So poor Mr. Woolly fails at the one thing everyone else believes he's supposed to accomplish every single year, but he keeps on doing what he knows he's supposed to do. Living a life that others might deem insignificant. He thaws out, wakes up, eats and freezes again…for fourteen years." Evan sent the plate full of garlic toast around the table.

"I don't know if caterpillars ponder about their purpose much, but if I was him I'd start to get discouraged and question things." He went to pick up the baking pan holding the asiago chicken, but yanked his hand away quickly. "That one's still hot. Pass your plates and I'll put some on there." He held out hands for both their plates. A fourth place setting was saved for Laura, who he said would be home shortly.

He served up the chicken and then handed back their plates. "But God does something amazing in Mr. Woolly's life every year. Woolly freezes solid and then comes back to life. I can't do that, you can't do that. It's a big deal. But Woolly doesn't know that because he's just being faithful."

Every year Woolly felt like he'd failed, yet he kept being faithful. Could Claire claim the same thing? Everyone else expected the caterpillar to change, to be more, but God had other plans for him—delayed plans—and there was something special about that. She pushed salad around on her plate. Sadness seeped through her chest. She shouldn't feel this emotional about a silly Arctic caterpillar.

"I have a theory that our lives are a lot like that." Evan leaned back in his chair, his food untouched. Maybe he was holding off for Laura. "We're waiting for this great thing that we want, but it's not going to happen for *fourteen more years*. All the while we're missing the very real and cool things God is doing in our lives right now."

Claire let her gaze fall to her cup of water

and studied the ice cubes floating inside. Anything to avoid eye contact with Evan and Alex, because she worried that if she did, they'd see right through her. They'd know that she was a frozen caterpillar who was afraid the thaw would never arrive.

Once Laura joined them for dinner Evan said a prayer and they all dug in. Evan wanted to circle the table and hug Laura because of the way she instantly charmed Claire's son. She was always dog tired when she got home from practice, but an outsider wouldn't have been able to tell. Laura listened enthusiastically as Alex rattled off the different types of bees in a hive and what their jobs were.

"A honeybee hive can produce twenty to eighty pounds of honey. Did you know that?" Alex hardly gave Laura time to answer before launching into a different topic.

After the table was cleared she challenged Alex to a board game. Evan whispered "thank you" and dropped a kiss on the top of her head.

Claire trailed him down the hallway toward the set of white painted French doors that led to his office. Did it bother her to leave Alex out of sight, with someone who wasn't a relative? "Laura does a lot of babysitting for families at church. She's good with kids his age."

"She's doing great with Alex. You both have a way with him." Claire touched Evan's elbow, stopping him before he went through the doors. She lowered her voice. "Alex has anger issues. Have you ever heard of attachment disorder?"

Laura and Alex were too far away to overhear them, and around the corner, so they couldn't even see the part of the hallway where Evan and Claire were huddled. Still, Evan inched closer to her so they could speak in a whisper. "I have."

"And you believe it's real? My dad doesn't."

Of course Sesser didn't. Anything the man viewed as weakness was deemed not good enough for him or his family. Poor Alex. Evan knew full well how much the brunt of Sesser's judgment could hurt. Destroy.

But attacking her dad wouldn't help the situation.

Evan raked his mind for a way to explain. "Have you forgotten about *my* dad?"

Claire ran her finger over the grooved frame around the door. Evan had created every single piece of woodwork in his house. She was absently tracing over hours of his handiwork. "I know he…he didn't treat you well."

"There's a reason he's not invited to my brother's wedding. He used to beat the tar out of Brice. He would come at me, but most of the time Brice put himself between me and him and took the worst of it." Evan applied pressure to the bridge of his nose. "So I've done some digging into childhood psychology. Brice and I both have, because when we became Christians we knew part of the process involved investing in mental and emotional health. It makes sense that Alex might have something like that, given his background."

"He seems to get along with you, though. He's mentioned you a couple times every day since we saw you last week at town hall."

"That's because I'm no threat to him." Evan let his hands fall to his sides. "He can talk to me on his terms and it means nothing if he loses my esteem. That's the reason he's open with me."

"I don't think that's the only reason. He doesn't talk to me *at all*. He never said a word about that woolly caterpillar to me." Claire looked up at the ceiling and swiped at her eyes. Was she crying over the insect story? "Why doesn't he tell me about those kinds of things?" She hugged her arms around her stomach and her shoulders hunched forward.

Evan had to do something. He couldn't stand there and watch her fight tears without trying to offer encouragement. So he reached over, cupped her arm and gave a companionable squeeze. "He has more to lose if he gets rejected by you."

"I won't reject him, though." She slapped a hand over her mouth. Her voice had gone up more than she'd meant it to.

"You know that, but he can't believe it yet. Give him time." Evan kept his hand on her arm as he walked her backward through the French doors. It was only when he had her in his office that he remembered the giant painting—her painting—hanging behind his desk.

Claire turned and froze. "You kept my painting."

All other sounds faded; she could hear only the pounding of blood in her temples. Her neck went uncomfortably warm.

Evan had her painting—her last gift to him.

She'd spent weeks layering the colors just right. She brushed past him now and rounded his desk to get a closer look. The painting had been a graduation gift. She'd given it to him only a few weeks before he'd ditched their wedding. Claire had always figured he'd sold it or tossed it or burned it in a bonfire. Never in any scenario that had played out in her head had she imagined him keeping the gift.

"I can't believe you kept it."

Evan cleared his throat. "I think it looks good in here." He hooked his hands into his pockets and rocked on his feet, clearly uncomfortable. "It fits."

"Why would you keep something like that, though?"

His eyes softened as they searched hers. "Claire, you told me before you didn't want to talk about the past, but can we now?" He motioned toward the picture. "I've wanted to explain."

Curiosity roared for an answer, but a bigger part of her heart, the piece that belonged to fear and remembered all the agony it had been through previously, whispered *no*. Ignorance was better than pain. Safer. She'd written to him; she'd begged for an explanation and he hadn't offered one then. Nothing he said now could ease the suffering she'd been dragged through, or fix how falling for him had sabotaged any chance of success for any other relationships. He couldn't take away the brand his betrayal had seared over her heart.

Unwanted.

Evan had been the only risk she'd taken in

life. One of only two times she'd attempted to cross her father. And what had she gotten from it? Evan had removed the safety net and then allowed her to fall to the ground, shattering.

She wasn't about to let that happen again.

She pressed her fingers to her forehead. "This was a bad idea. I don't know why I'm here."

He caught her wrist as she turned. "Hey, slow down. You're here because we have a fund-raiser to plan and very little time to do it in." He pointed toward the painting. "You don't want to talk about what this means, that's fine. Like I told you before, I'll respect that. So let's forget about it and get to planning."

"Just like that?"

"Claire, you deserve more in this life than I could ever give you. The *least* I can do is honor your wishes."

It was strange, how much could be accomplished when tension breathed down their necks like a pack of wolves. Claire kept her eyes off her painting as much as she could and tried to focus. Evan had his laptop open and took notes as they brainstormed. They settled on hosting a 5k walk/run with a bake sale at the end.

Evan paused over his keyboard. "We could do something like a doughnut-eating contest at the finish of the race."

Claire scrunched up her face. "Right after running? People will throw up."

He folded his hands behind his head and tossed his feet onto his desk, leaning back. "Which would be quality entertainment."

"I beg to differ."

"I'm joking." He let his feet fall back to the floor and the chair righted again. "Well, not about the doughnuts. Pastries aren't a laughing matter."

Claire tapped her temple. "I'll tuck that nugget away for future reference."

He barked a laugh and moved back over to his keyboard. "I know a guy who owns a bakery in Shadowbend. I'm pretty sure I can get him to donate everything so it wouldn't eat into our costs. The contest could be open to anyone, not just runners from the 5k. That way, it makes our event more appealing to a broader audience."

Claire jotted "doughnuts" onto the pad of paper she was working on. "Talk to your guy. If he'll do it for free, why not?"

"Let me make sure my notes are right and then I'll email them to you. No arguments. If

I know you, that sheet of paper you're working on will become a crumpled ball at the bottom of your purse within the next hour."

She ripped the page off the memo pad and folded it four times. "I'm afraid you're right."

"Okay." He squinted at the glowing screen. "I'm in charge of talking to my friend Miles at the police department about approval for the racecourse, and you're calling the organization that times these things to see if there's anything else we need in order for this all to be official."

"Sounds perfect."

He pointed at her even though his focus was fixed on the computer screen. "You'll call your mom's country-club friends and get a list of donors started for the bake sale, and I'm going to make calls to the church ladies for the same reason."

This was the Evan that his followers from high school had never seen—studious, organized, ready to take on the world for good. The popular kids had wanted to peg him as the handsome jokester or the ladies' man, but he'd never truly been those things. He was an all-in kind of guy. When he built something or helped someone, every cell in his body was dedicated to that purpose. Right here in his office, bent over a project, was the real Evan Daniels.

Inches away...the Evan she'd loved still existed.

And that was the most painful part. This moment. The realization that had just stabbed through her was why she hadn't wanted to return to Goose Harbor.

She had to get out of here. "You forgot something on the list." Her voice carried a false cheerfulness she didn't possess at the moment.

Evan poised his fingers over his keyboard. "I'm ready. Hit me with it."

"You missed the part where it's late and we have to build snowmen tomorrow."

The community email blast penned by Mr. Banks had announced that they would kick off the mayoral competition with the first test beginning at noon in the square. He'd called it a snow festival, even though she and Evan building snow sculptures was the only pre-planned event.

Evan nodded and closed his laptop. "Our creativity on display for all to see." He eased around the desk and held out his hand to her. "What are you making?"

She feigned being busy with her purse so

she could politely ignore his gesture as she rose. "That's a well-guarded secret."

He buried his hands in the pockets of his hooded sweatshirt and glanced at the clock. "Oh, wow. It's past ten thirty."

"What? Alex should have been to bed hours ago."

Evan followed her out of the office. Laura and Alex were both snoring in the living room, light from the television screen casting shadows over their faces. A movie with talking animals played in the background. No doubt Laura had searched the display until she found something age appropriate for Alex. Claire made a mental note to thank her for being so thoughtful tonight. There were a million more exciting ways she could have spent her Saturday night. Maybe Claire would pick the teenager up a gift card for one of the local shops.

Soft breaths whooshed out of Alex's parted lips. His brow, which was bunched with frustration so much of the time, was completely relaxed. Claire's fingers twitched; she itched to smooth back his hair. Kiss his temple. Whisper that he was her son and she loved him, that he never had to fear being unwanted or rejected ever again.

"I hate to wake him." She worked her lip between her teeth.

"Don't." Evan held up a hand and shuffled forward. He bent and lifted Alex, immediately making for the door. "Grab his coat," he whispered. "See if you can get it on him without waking him."

Evan held Alex as Claire slipped his arms into his down jacket. Should she zip it up? She decided against it, fearing it would cause him to stir. Next she grabbed her coat and tugged her heavy boots on before turning back to Evan. "You don't have a coat on or shoes." Ugh. She sounded like such a *mom*. Evan was a grown man. She added, with slightly less authority in her voice, "At least let me help you step into some boots."

"I don't want to trip."

She opened her mouth to protest.

"I'll be fine," Evan said.

In only socks?

Grown man, Claire. Let him be.

She held the door open and he followed her out. A hiss passed from his lips when he stepped into the yard. The cold bite of winter prickled against her cheeks. She could only imagine how freezing Evan's feet must be. The snow would soak through his socks instantly. She unlocked her car and held the door open for him as he set Alex into his booster seat. Claire slid forward so she could reach and buckle him in. When she turned around, Evan was still behind her, one hand resting on the top of her car and the other slung over the open door.

She glanced back at Alex. "He'll get cold."

Without a word, Evan slipped his arm around her waist and drew her out of the door opening. With his arm circling her there was no comfortable place to put her free hand other than his chest. Despite the temperature and his lack of a coat and shoes, Evan was acting as if he wasn't chilled at all. In fact, the intensity in his gaze sent warmth curling through Claire. He closed the car door but kept his hold on her.

Dim light spilled from the large front windows of his house, enough to show his beautiful green eyes, which were only a breath away from hers. Searching her face. What was he looking for?

"Do you still paint?"

Of all the things for him to ask her right now...

Claire had loved art and once dreamed of becoming an artist, opening a studio in town. Evan had encouraged her passion for drawing and painting, but her parents had berated her for wasting time on something so frivolous. Hardly anyone made a living from art.

She swallowed hard. "Not since…not in a long time."

His face contorted for a second. Maybe from standing in the snow without shoes on. Served him right.

"Why do you care?" Claire whispered. A stiff wind caught her hair and sent it dancing around them.

As if he was mapping out a long journey or searching the sky for an undiscovered star, Evan's gaze traced from her hair to her eyes to her lips, and back to her eyes. "The world was richer when you did."

"Painting doesn't—"

"When you're doing something you love…" He shook his head and let his arms slip away. "Take care, Claire-bear."

Then he was gone, leaving her with nothing but an old nickname that tore her heart in two.

Chapter Seven

The crowd gathered in the square to watch the snow sculpture competition was easily three or four times bigger than Claire had expected, especially when the snowfall was taken into consideration.

At some point while they were all sleeping the skies had opened and dumped even more snow onto their little section of the world. The drive to church was somewhat treacherous, but now that it was later in the day the public works crews had all the roads cleared.

Board members had set up roped-off areas on either side of the square, one for Evan and one for Claire. The only rule was that the snow sculptures had to be ready for judging by six that evening.

Some people had brought sleeping bags or wore snow pants, signaling that they were in for the long haul. Once again, Claire had to admit that the board and Evan were both right—as ridiculous as the competitions were, the people of Goose Harbor needed this distraction.

A troop of school-aged entrepreneurs sold hot chocolate, three flavors of coffee and a few tea options from a card table near the gazebo, and Jenna and Toby Holcomb, along with their daughter, Kasey, were working through the crowd with boxes of cinnamon doughnut holes, freshly made at the industrial kitchen at their apple orchard. Despite it being Sunday, many of the shops along the square were open.

With two large throwaway cups in her hands, Kendall picked her way through the crowd toward Claire. She handed her one. "Vanilla rooibos latte. From Kay's Kitchen." Kendall jutted her head to indicate the diner that had only recently opened. "I know you love the coffee at Tradewinds, but this stuff is amazing. Trust me."

"As long as you promise this thing has caffeine in it—" Claire jiggled the cup "—I'm happy."

"Then drink and be happy, my friend." Kendall took a long sip of her latte and smacked her lips. "So what's the plan here?"

Claire sighed as she examined the gigantic mound of snow one of the public works trucks had dumped into her taped-off area. The heat from the cup warmed her hand. "Build a snowman, I guess. I mean, how hard can it—"

A round of applause cut off her words. The largest concentration of people were gathered around Evan's area, blocking the sight line. Kendall craned her neck to get a better view.

"Are they seriously applauding his arrival?" Claire gaped at the crowd.

Kendall shrugged. "This town loves that man."

"Oh, come on, let's just go over there." Claire playfully smacked her friend in the arm. "I should scope out my competition, anyway."

Evan was unloading tool after tool from the bed of his truck. Three plastic garbage cans, a few plastic totes, an ice-fishing auger, five different shaped saws and a shovel... In spite of the temperature, he wasn't wearing a coat. Instead he had on work jeans and heavy boots and what appeared to be three or four layers of long-sleeved shirts. The sleeves on each were rolled in a way that looked effortlessly stylish. While everyone else—including Claire—waddled around like fluffy T. rexes in their large puffer coats.

"Oh, brother." Claire spun around and marched back to her snow pile. Evan knew how to put on a show, how to play to an audience. No matter what she did today, he would outshine her. That was his way. He did it without trying.

What she wouldn't give for a thimbleful of his confidence.

But they were different. Evan didn't have to navigate his life or weigh other people's attention based on what they could use him for. He wasn't a pawn to be played for personal gain like she'd been. He was judged and liked for who he was—his own merits, his personhood. He had never had to struggle with trying to live up to impossible standards.

What must that be like?

She heard the bang of Evan closing his tailgate, and soon after that the crowd began to disperse, moving like an amoeba toward the shops and eating areas in search of somewhere warm to lie low for a few hours. People would be able to come and go at their leisure throughout the day to check on Evan's and Claire's progress.

Kendall jogged to catch up to her. "You have to admit, he's adorable."

"You do know you're going to be related to him, right?"

"Ew." Kendall's lips curled into a hilarious caricature of disgust. "I so didn't mean it like that. And you know that! Brice is much more my style." She did a whole-body shiver and stomped her feet, trying to get warm.

Claire jammed her latte onto a small table that had been set up in her area and lodged a boot into the mountain of snow that she was supposed to make something out of. "The main problem with Evan Daniels is—"

"That he's standing right behind you." Evan's voice stopped her in her tracks.

Kendall let out a low whistle and backed away.

Claire slowly faced him.

He flashed a full-dimpled smile. "Wait. Let me guess. Is it that I can't reach the center of my back when I have an itch? Because I'm pretty sure that's a fairly common problem for most humans."

It's that you're some force of nature. You can't help people falling for you.

Anything she'd wanted to say about him became lodged in her throat.

Evan tugged off his glove. "I only came over to shake hands before we started. Good sportsmanship and all that." He extended his hand.

She took it. "Aren't you cold?"

He pursed his lips and wagged his head, lowering his voice as if he was sharing a great secret. "Thermal underwear. Pretty standard issue for us outdoorsmen."

"You're hardly an outdoorsman."

Their hands were still clasped together. A camera clicked. Another.

"I build furniture all winter long in my garage with the door cracked. That's outdoor-*ish*." He tilted his head, questioning.

"Totally doesn't count." She jerked her chin toward his area of the square. "What's with all the stuff you dragged from your truck? Just for show?"

"Highly technical snow sculpting equipment." He tugged on her hand, bringing her closer. "I watched some how-to videos online last night. We'll see how it goes."

Evan pushed his hands into his lower back and leaned against them, stretching aching muscles. His fingers were going numb, but he needed to continue working.

Skylar Ashby stepped gingerly into his roped-off area. "Dad said to give you these." She handed him two pocket warmers.

He groaned with joy and slipped them into the palms of his gloves. "Thank him for me." Evan curled his fingers into the heat. *Wow*, that felt good. "I was afraid my fingers were going to fall off soon."

She held her elbow in one hand and her chin in the other, examining his almost completed sculpture. Admittedly, he'd gone a little overboard. There was a six-foot-tall goose with its wings spread wide. He'd had to reinforce the goose's neck and legs with planks he'd stowed in the back of his truck. Under one of the bird's wings was a smaller sculpture of a kid sledding down a hill, and he was working on a boat for the other side but didn't know if he'd have enough time to finish. Snow wasn't a difficult medium for him, after working with wood for so many years. It was more like clay or dough once he added some water to it.

"It's not half-bad," Skylar offered. "But I bet my dad could have made something cooler."

Evan bit back a smile. "Your dad is your hero, isn't he?"

She nodded and ducked her head a little in an uncharacteristic display of embarrassment.

She toed at a pile of snow he'd shaved off from his sculpture. "Actually, he probably wouldn't have built anything as good as you. That's your gift, not his. Maggie says everyone has one. She's good at feeding people—not just with food. She feeds you here, too." Skylar tapped her heart. Maggie and Kellen hadn't been married long, but the girls' love for their stepmom was evident.

"My dad is better with words. How he writes songs and leads worship and sometimes what he says…it makes you feel a lot of things." Skylar walked a circle around Evan's sculptures, examining them from every angle. "Your gift is building."

She made the declaration with a certainty that caused nervous energy to race down his neck.

"Thanks, Sky." He coughed to clear his throat. "I like to make things."

"But Maggie says you can't just use your gift for you. She says you have to ask yourself how does my gift help others? And how does God want me to use my gift? I know you make stuff for church and help people, and everyone knows you're the one who built the ramp for the Turner family when Miss Nancy had to go into a wheelchair."

So much for doing things anonymously.

His hands had thawed enough, so Evan pulled the pocket warmers out of his gloves.

"Maggie and my dad, both their gifts change people on the inside. Dad says people are forever, so they're what matter the most." She popped her hands to her hips. "Do you think that, too?"

He braced his elbows on his knees as he crouched to be eye level with her. "I do."

She cocked her head and pulled a face as if she was figuring out a math puzzle. "So do you build people?"

"Nope, I think that's God's job." He sank one of his hands to the ground for balance.

"But you *could* build people up. That's your gift."

His legs were starting to tire, so he dropped to his knees. "I guess I never thought about it that way before."

"I think my gift is being smart." Skylar boxed the sides of her face between her gloved hands. "But my brain hurts now. I just used up all my smarts on you."

That made him throw back his head and laugh. "I'm sorry I drained all your brainpower. I must be an especially difficult case."

She nodded gravely in agreement. "I'm going to take a break from thinking. Breaks are okay with God, right?"

"Definitely." Evan pushed up to his feet again. He dusted snow off his jeans. "And

Sky?" he called after her retreating figure. "I think your gift is being smart, too."

With only an hour left in the competition, Evan began collecting his tools and packing them back into his truck. He'd leave the square free of any debris besides snow.

Mrs. Clarkson stopped by and demanded he stand beside the goose so she could snap a few pictures. "This is really a lovely event. I'm going to petition the board to host an annual snow festival every year. How'd you build the snow up enough to carve it?"

"I covered the inside of the trash cans with car wax this morning so I could pack the snow in there and then add water. Then when you turn it over it comes out easily and stays together. Same as using forms to build a sand castle."

"You are one talented young man."

He plastered on a smile, but it felt disingenuous. He wasn't anything special, just a guy who'd stayed up long after his bedtime watching videos on his phone to pick up some pointers. If he hadn't…he'd be struggling. His gaze trailed to where Claire was pushing over another one of her snowmen. Her frustrated grunt echoed through the square. She was giving up—getting rid of all her work.

She needed help.

You could build people up.

Did it go against the rules for one candidate to help another?

Do. Not. Cry.

Claire sucked in frigid gulps of air, letting the cold jolt her lungs. All she had to show for four hours of work were three lopsided snowmen in different sizes. She'd pushed down a few more out of frustration and was considering the demise of the ones in front of her, too.

Returning to Goose Harbor had been a mistake. She'd never felt that more than in this moment. She didn't belong here. Didn't fit.

At least when she was in New York she could blend in a little better. No one thought much of a wealthy man's daughter hobnobbing at studio openings or curating priceless art collections. Wealthy families were a dime a dozen in that world.

But in Goose Harbor she got a front page spread in the newspaper dedicated to her campaign because Dad owned the paper. She had a well-paid position within his company that meant she barely had to accomplish any real work in order to find a direct deposit waiting in her account. Yet she didn't have a career. It was Dad's money that had funded

Alex's adoption. She had a bunch of advanced degrees that looked great hanging on a wall, but had forfeited *living* in order to get them.

Her parents had drilled the importance of success into her head at an early age.

If you hang out with those kids they'll bring you down, and you can't afford to have people thinking less of you. Don't join that club—it won't help get you into a good college. Stop spending so much time painting, but spend it on things that matter, like your grade point average. Those people are trying to be your friend only to get at my money. They're using you, sweetheart.

What if following their advice had cost her any chance at happiness?

By her parents' standards Evan was unsuccessful. He wasn't college educated and had no experience outside of their small town. But Evan was rich in the things that mattered. He had friends and people who cared about him; he was loved and valued. He'd built a business with his own two hands—literally—and had turned it into a profitable and satisfying career. Evan loved his work and the things he built. He had a home of his own. He'd made a place for himself in this community, and if he left, the whole town would feel his absence.

If Claire disappeared no one would notice.

She fisted her hands and glared at her snowmen. Maybe she should push them all over and forfeit the competition completely.

God, why did You let my life turn out this way? What did I do wrong? How come I never fit in? I'm thirty and I'm still so...lost. Why can't I, just once, matter to someone— for me? Please, show me how to live. I need help. I don't know how to do this on my own.

"Please tell me you're not plotting any more snowman murders." Evan's voice. Of course.

She opened her eyes, not that she remembered closing them, and pressed her teeth together so hard her jaw hurt.

"I'm sorry I didn't make it in time to perform hostage negotiations for that one." He tapped the little snowman-shaped mound with the toe of his shoe.

Tired and sick of being out in the elements, she crossed her arms in front of her chest. "Did you come over here to gloat?"

"No, like I said, hostage negotiations." He inched forward to place his body between her and her snowmen, then put his arms out to block her access to them. "Please, they don't deserve such a brutal end."

He was joking. Just trying to get her to

laugh, but she wasn't sure she wanted to be cheered up.

Just go away. "I'm really not in the mood." She tore off her gloves and tossed them onto the table. "Clearly, you won. Congratulations. Sorry I don't have confetti to throw in the air. Want a faceful of snow instead?"

"Claire-bear—"

"Do not use that name." She whirled and rammed her pointer finger into the center of his chest. "You lost the right to call me that a long time ago."

He frowned, kicked at the ground. "It slipped out."

"Whatever. I'm done." She snatched her gloves off the table and shoved them into her pockets. "There's no point staying for the judging." She had to get out of here before she broke down. It had come too close to that when she was praying. "If this is what this town wants in a mayor I'm obviously not who they're going to pick, so—"

"Enough." He caught her by the crook of her arm and pulled her close. "You're not a coward. Stop giving up. Stop choosing defeat."

"Believe me. I do not *choose* it."

"You do." There was a growl in his voice. "You're doing it now and you've done it every time you've refused to let me explain about the past."

Digging her elbow into his ribs until he winced, she yanked away from him. "How dare you—"

He sidestepped, blocking her retreat so she almost slammed into his chest. He took hold of her shoulders. "The Claire I knew and loved had the fire to match her hair. *That* Claire would never give up this easily. She was this remarkable woman who would use the amazing talents she'd been blessed with and would wow everyone." He released her, turning to the side. His hand landed in his hair and he tugged on the ends. "I miss her so much."

Oh, she wanted to toss back an angry barb. Wanted to fuel the fight so she wouldn't have to deal with the truth of what he had said. Get under his skin as much as he'd quickly been able to get under hers.

Coward.

Only moments ago she'd asked God to help her. What if Evan's words were an answer to her prayer? It would be easier, less terrifying, to shrug him off and tell him to mind his own business. To throw in his face that he'd abandoned her and therefore she couldn't trust him and he had no right to miss her. But if she truly wanted to learn to live, that would take change and risks and honesty.

"I don't know what to do." Her voice was hoarse.

"Claire." He scrubbed his hand over his jaw, then up his neck. "What do you love?"

You.

Her stomach tightened as an anxious feeling rolled through it.

That couldn't be right. She didn't—couldn't—love Evan Daniels. Not still. Not now.

Yet the way he was looking at her, believed in her, was rooting for her to win even though he was the one she would beat… She loved him. The man at her side was everything she'd fallen for in high school, only amplified.

"Do what you love, Claire. Find that, and do it. I just want you to be happy."

He'd said something similar last night when he'd asked if she still painted. *The world was richer when you did.*

She looked up and her gaze landed on The Craft Shack, a tiny store filled with art supplies squeezed between two restaurants on the square. It forever smelled like a mix of tacos and Italian beef inside.

"Evan." She latched on to his arm, jiggled it. "Evan!" More jiggling. She pointed toward the store with her other hand. "You're a genius!"

"You've got forty minutes." He propelled her in the direction of The Craft Shack. "Go." He pushed on her back gently. "Move."

She tore through the square and across the brick road at a full-out sprint. The bells hanging at the entrance of the craft store performed a samba when she exploded through the door. With frozen fingers she pawed through her pockets until she located one of her credit cards. "Paint." She dropped the card onto the counter. "I need tons of paint. Quick. And these." She scooped brushes and cups and other supplies into her arms.

Minutes later she was squatting on the ground, painting murals all over the snowmen she hadn't pushed over when she was considering giving up. A crowd gathered behind her, whispering excitedly. Evan caught her eye and sent her a thumbs-up.

"Mr. Daniels!" Mr. Banks waved his arms as if he was landing a plane. The man wore a bright green, head-to-toe snowsuit, as if he was out skiing.

Evan crossed his eyes for Claire's benefit and then acknowledged Mr. Banks, so that the man would stop flapping his arms.

"Your goose is cooked." Mr. Banks puffed

out a breath. "The head fell off." He pointed across the square.

Evan grimaced. "It appears I have some hostage negotiations of my own to deal with."

Chapter Eight

A shrill electronic beep let Evan know that someone had entered his store. He'd hooked up the sensor after one too many customers sneaked up on him while he was working. Evan maneuvered his protective glasses to the top of his head and clapped his hands twice to clear away any remaining sawdust.

The store was divided into two sections: one was for finished items, and the other side was set up as a workshop. There was no point in him sitting at a counter all day when he could be building.

Goose Harbor Furniture, the shop he owned, was on a small path just off the square. He shared the building with his soon-to-be sister-in-law's business. Needless to say, now that Brice had a very pretty reason to come into town, Evan saw his brother more than usual. So he wasn't too surprised when Brice barreled in.

Evan unhooked his heavy tool belt and laid it on the counter. "If you're coming to remind me about your rehearsal dinner again, I know. Thursday—tomorrow night. Agostini's." He tapped his forehead. "I remember." He left the work space to join his brother in the showroom area of the shop.

Brice was pacing back and forth in front of a dining set. Prewedding nerves?

"I'll be at the wedding on Friday night, too." Evan stretched, his spine letting out a series of pops. "Even though I have a 5k to run the next morning."

Sign-ups were going well for the Valentine's Day Shuffle that Evan and Claire had spent the last week and a half planning. The whole process had been easier than he'd anticipated. A few meetings with board members and the police department had gotten the running course approved, while Mr. Banks's latest email blast, a post on the town website and an article in the paper served as marketing. People had flocked to town hall during business hours to register for the run, the bake sale and the eating contest. The ladies at church had swooped in and plucked the details of the bake sale right out of their hands.

And Claire and Evan had gladly relinquished planning it. Part of leadership was knowing when to delegate, after all.

Brice stopped pacing, tugged off his baseball hat and crushed it in his hands. "Do you have internet connection in here?"

He jutted his thumb toward the wall he shared with Kendall. "I steal it from your fiancée."

"Evan…" Brice growled.

"What? Her password was way too easy." It rhymed with *trice* and had their wedding date. Not exactly rocket science. "We're going to be family. Think of me as the crazy uncle who borrows a piece of silverware every time you host a party until you have none left."

Brice worked his jaw back and forth. "We have an uncle like that."

"Uncle Ernie." Evan bobbed his head. "Weird guy. I'm still not a hundred percent sure if he's related to us by blood or if he's just one of Dad's old gambling buddies."

Brice tilted his head. "Whatever happened to him?"

Evan thought for a moment and then snapped his fingers. "Didn't he marry a retired shot-putter? She came with him once. Her biceps were bigger than my head. It was amazing." Evan held up his hands to demonstrate the size. "She was from some country that started with an A. Algeria? I think that's probably wrong."

"Living the life," Brice deadpanned.

"With our silverware."

Ah. There. Finally. He'd wheedled a grin out of his brother.

It faded just as quickly.

Brice produced a crumpled piece of paper from his wallet and laid it on the counter. He pointed to a long internet address written in his uneven script. "Pull up this website."

Evan typed it into his laptop and a popular blog site loaded. The page displayed a header showing Lake Michigan with some boats on it. Clearly a shot taken from their pier.

Evan read the title. *Goose Tales*. "Since when do you read gossip blogs?"

"You've heard of *Goose Tales*?"

The blog had been steadily updated for the past two years. Whoever ran it would post about someone who was selling subpar fruit at the farmers' market or announce the closing of a business before the news was official. Evan had a hard time taking an anonymous writer seriously, no matter how salacious their stories became.

"Everyone in Goose Harbor who doesn't live under a rock knows about it. Rumors,

Brice. That's all this blog is. Someone with too much time on their hands who makes a bigger deal about issues or straight-up invents them." He wouldn't be surprised if the author was Mr. Banks or someone along those lines.

Evan scanned the latest story and spotted photos of him and Claire together at the snow sculpture contest. A couple were fairly good shots. He might save them to his computer.

"For the last week they've been detailing you and Claire." Brice delivered the statement as if it was groundbreaking information. Kendall had done wonders to lighten his brother's overall attitude, but a lot of Brice's characteristic grumpy-bear personality would always be there. That was a good thing though because Evan liked his brother that way.

"We're running for office. That seems like a given."

Brice elbowed him out of the way so he could squint at the screen. "Supposedly they have proof that the two of you are in cahoots over the election."

"Which you know isn't true. Side note." Evan held up a hand to pause the conversation. "Who uses the word *cahoots*?"

Brice scrolled to older posts, which displayed screenshots of some of the photos Jason had captured of them for use on the town's webpage. "A lot of these pictures make it look like what's written here is true. You two look like a couple."

"How about next time I see Claire, I'll scowl at her the entire time. That would make a better photo, right?"

Brice ignored his egging. "Tonight's the math challenge."

"Ugh." The problem-solving portion of the competition. "Don't remind me."

Evan glanced at the clock. Twenty minutes until he was supposed to show up in the high school gym so he could sit at a table and take a math quiz while his neighbors watched.

"You build things for a living. That makes you inherently good at math."

"Good at *some* math," Evan clarified. "The practical kind. Not the kind that goes 'Jane is on a train going twice as fast as Timmy's train, but only three times as fast as Lenny's. If Lenny has two oranges and Jane has five, but throws one out the window, what color shirt is Timmy wearing?'"

"It's called a word problem."

"If those are on the test, I'm going to sketch pictures of sharks instead. Maybe they'll up my creativity points from Sunday."

His brother closed the laptop and removed

the drawer from the cash register. "So you're going to hand this win to Claire, too?"

"I didn't *hand* her the last challenge." Evan took the cash drawer and put it in the safe. He went to lock up the front door. They were already past closing time. "My goose crumbled seconds before the judges showed. These challenges are all about entertainment, anyway. I'm not that concerned about winning them."

"What about the actual position?" Brice leaned against the counter and folded his arms over his chest. His brother was built like a house, wide and strong. If Evan didn't know that Brice was really an easy pushover, he'd make an intimidating image. "Are you still concerned with winning that?"

Evan sighed. The only reason he was in the election at all was because Brice had told him to do it. He'd do anything for his brother. After the childhood they'd had together, he owed it to Brice. In the past Evan had given up everything for him. Not that Brice knew that, nor would he ever if it was up to Evan.

But he could at least come clean about the race. "Honest answer?"

"Of course."

He took a deep breath and let his words

spill out in a rush. "I never cared about winning it. I'm running because you told me to."

"You want what's best for this town. You care about it. She doesn't."

"How do you know she doesn't care?"

"Sesser—"

"She's not her father. When are you going to get that through your head? She's not out to be his minion."

Brice disliked the man more than Evan did, which was difficult to top. But Brice allowed his feelings concerning Sesser to color his reasoning when it came to Claire. He'd never approved of Evan's relationship with her. Brice had been at college when she and Evan dated. Evan needed his brother to understand that Claire was different than Sesser. If there was one thing she wanted, it was to be known for herself, not her association with her dad.

"Claire's smart. She puts others first. She wants the best for this town because this is where she's raising her son." When his brother didn't speak, Evan added, "Maybe it's not so bad if she wins."

"I can't believe this." Brice started pacing again. Never a good sign.

"I hate disappointing you. I just—"

Brice speared him with a look of disbelief. "You love her again. It came back."

Evan couldn't deny it. He'd realized how he felt the night Alex and Claire had come for dinner. When he'd helped them out to their car he hadn't wanted to let them go. They belonged at his house. With him.

At least, that's what kept running through his head.

Not that it mattered. He'd never act on those thoughts. Stepping into Claire's life would only cause her pain, like before. Her parents didn't like him. Besides, Claire still refused to talk to him about their past. If she wasn't even willing to have that conversation, they could never move forward. Hurt didn't heal by ignoring it.

Evan slumped against the wall. "Was it ever gone? I mean, yeah, I shoved it away and told myself I wasn't allowed to care. But…" He tossed his hands up and gave an exaggerated shrug. He loved Claire. "Don't worry. Claire and I…we would never work."

Brice nodded. "It would be close to impossible, the Danielses and the Atwoods."

"Water and oil."

Claire covered the smile blooming on her face as she watched Evan march up and down the hallway outside the gymnasium. Banks had explained that they were to stay tucked away until he announced them.

She peered through the narrow window in a door. Two sets of bleachers were pulled out and residents filled most of the seats. Alex and his friend Kasey were dancing with a group of other children around someone dressed as the school mascot, Jaws the Gator. Gator Pride, a concession stand built into the side of the gym, had a line of people waiting for drinks and the lukewarm hot dogs they sold. The sweet smells of fresh cotton candy and brewing coffee formed an oddly pleasant aroma when mingled together.

Evan continued to pace.

Claire shook her head. "You're going to wear a groove into the floor if you don't stop that."

He chuckled and rubbed his chin. With a sigh he sagged back against a locker, one foot propped against the metal. And that quickly, he was the teenage boy she'd fallen for, leaning in the same hallway where they'd walked together, flashing a dimpled smile meant only for her.

Despite his happy demeanor, his gaze was faraway, distracted. "Do you read the gossip blog?"

"Like the ones about celebrities?"

"No." He folded his arms. "The Goose Harbor one."

Goose Tales. Of course.

"You mean the one my dad is on a tirade about?" If she'd thought her father had overreacted about the photos Jason had taken to announce her and Evan as candidates, he'd almost lost his mind when he'd discovered the updates from the anonymous blog. Last night he'd slammed every door in the house and kept repeating that it had been a mistake for her to come home. *How come you couldn't have married Pierce and been done with all of this? Why couldn't you have done that one, simple thing?*

"Brice, too."

Evan's brother and she had formed a tenuous relationship for Kendall's benefit. Claire would stand in their wedding on Friday, and always encourage Kendall and speak well about the man her friend loved. But Brice hung back from Claire whenever they were in the same room. She couldn't work out if it was because he was somewhat shy or if it was more personal. It often felt the latter. He didn't like her father—that was common knowledge—but was there more to it?

"Brice doesn't like me much, does he?"

"I don't think that's the case. Only he's invested in seeing me win." Evan straightened and clapped his hands together before stalking to the gym doors. "Why is Banks still talking? I wish he'd call our names and get it over with."

"Nervous?"

"Back in the day, I used to copy off your exams. Think they'd still let me do that?"

He'd talked his way out of plenty of detentions for that kind of behavior.

Claire shouldn't encourage him, but she couldn't help the comfort she found in joking around with Evan. "Mrs. Ottley is still the head of the math block and her eyesight's even worse than when we were students. You might be able to pull it off."

He peered through one of the windows. "Too bad about those two hundred people on the bleachers who might notice."

She followed him. Touched his elbow to get his attention. "Thank you," she said softly. "For yesterday. You deserved to win."

She'd only built snowmen—half of which she'd shoved over in frustration when she was contemplating giving up on the competition. But Evan had saved her from collapsing the last three and she'd had enough time to paint murals depicting Goose Harbor all over them.

They'd turned out pretty, but Evan had created a huge, beautiful sculpture. Even though it had broken minutes before the judging, he still should have won.

He batted his hand. "Your snow painting was great. You may want to take up the new medium."

She walked her fingers from his elbow down to his hand and squeezed it. "I wouldn't have done it without you."

Evan, her hero, her encourager. The one person who looked at her and saw her, even better than she saw and understood herself.

Evan glanced at their hands together. He traced his thumb over her knuckles. "We make a pretty good team, don't we?"

Mr. Banks called their names over the loudspeaker. Their cue.

There was a sadness in his sigh. "Too bad we're running against each other."

Chapter Nine

"Alex, please don't do this. Not now," Claire pleaded. The high heels she had planned to wear to Brice and Kendall's rehearsal dinner still dangled in her hands. "I have to head out. I'm already so late."

"I don't care." In one swoop he shoved everything off their coffee table, and one of Claire's glass art pieces she'd picked up while studying in Hong Kong smashed onto the hardwood floor with a giant crash. Glass exploded and popped all around the room, glittering across the floor, spelling out the warpath of an angry seven-year-old.

A seven-year-old she would never be able to reach. Who wouldn't accept her love or comfort. Her own son.

"Stay there." She held up a hand. "I don't want you to get cut."

Tears coursed down his cheeks, but he made no sound, no gesture to show he'd heard her other than standing still. Claire set her shoes on the rose fabric of one of the chairs and cautiously tiptoed through the mess to the kitchen in order the fetch the broom and dustpan. It took her ten minutes to sweep a safe path to Alex. How could she get him to see that she was willing to do the same thing in his life—create a path for him to safely navigate?

"Come on." She held out her hand. She'd deal with the rest of the mess later tonight, after she got home from the dinner. It was already planned that Alex would crash in one of her parents' guest rooms for the night, seeing as she'd have to be up with the birds the next morning to help with wedding day festivities.

Head down, Alex followed the cleared path, but sidestepped her hand. Without exchanging words they proceeded to the front door of their living area. Alex grabbed his backpack and Claire scooped up her purse, shoes and some other odds and ends. She opened the door and ushered Alex out into a hallway in her parents' house.

After she broke off her engagement to Auden and returned home, her parents had renovated a part of the east wing of their mansion to accommodate a separate living area for her. That part of the house had consisted of guest suites that no one ever used. It didn't matter how many times she had asked her parents not to alter the family home, or assured them she'd be able to get a job and find her own living situation. They were determined to lock her away in their house as if she was some shamed spinster. Once Mom and Dad got an idea into their heads, there was no point in trying to reason with them. So she'd relented. *Hey, the rent was free.*

Claire padded down the plush white carpeting, directing Alex to the part of the house where her mother spent most of her time—a sitting room off the kitchen where she was forever perched on the sofa in her curlers, watching one of the shopping networks. She made weekly outrageous purchases that showed up in box after endless box at their doorstep. Mom often feigned innocence about placing the orders, but her name and credit card were linked to every purchase. Suffice it to say, they would never run out of random kitchen gadgets.

Alex followed Claire down the stairs. His book bag dangled from his hands, so his knees hit it with every step. "I didn't mean for the art to break."

Claire gripped the railing and stopped. "I know."

He took that as his signal to sit on a step midway down the staircase. "Do you have to go tonight?"

He'd been repeating the same question for the last hour as she was getting ready, which made no sense. The entire rest of the day he'd spent locked in his room ignoring her, even when she'd tried to hang out with him. Her invitation to play a board game this morning had been met with a snort.

Claire shifted the bracelets around her wrist. "I'm the maid of honor at the wedding tomorrow. Rehearsal dinners come with the territory."

He skewed his face. "Territory?"

"I'm sorry, that's a tough word." It was easy to forget that English wasn't his first language and he was still learning. "Um, I should have said it's part of the responsibility you take on when you agree to stand up in a friend's wedding. But, hey, you get to come tomorrow. The Holcombs will pick you up and you can sit with them during the ceremony and reception."

"Not with you?"

"Sorry. I have to stand up front, alone. That's part of the rules."

"Not that I want to sit with you." Alex curved his hand over the railing and pulled himself up again. He slung the backpack over his shoulder and plowed down the rest of the stairs, looking almost like an angst-filled teenager and not the little boy in the picture she'd fallen in love with during the adoption process. The little boy he very much still was underneath all that pain and frustration. Grief and anger aged people.

She caught up to him. "Will you be okay with my mom tonight?" Now wasn't the time to push the word *grandma* on him.

"She let me play with the Slicetasic last time. She gives me guacamole and chips. They're delicious."

While Claire wanted to focus on why her seven-year-old was playing with one of Mom's kitchen gadgets, she had bigger issues to deal with at the moment. Besides, she knew her mother would never do that without supervising him. More than likely, Alex was exaggerating to solicit a reaction.

Claire got in front of him and blocked his progress into the kitchen. "Then I'd like to talk about what happened back in our apartment."

His dark hair fell so it shadowed his soulful eyes. "I don't want to."

"Alex." She took a half step closer and reached out to him. He flinched and her stomach performed a nosedive. Claire let her hand fall to her side. "I love you." Emotion thickened her voice. "You're my son for life, no matter what. You understand that, don't you?"

He kept his gaze glued to the floor. "Can I go find your mom?"

"Why were you so angry?"

"Dunno." He scuffed his shoe along a color variation in the travertine tiles. "Sometimes I just am."

She fought the urge to put her hands on his shoulders and give him a gentle shake. The contact wouldn't help. He wasn't receptive at the moment. "I couldn't even reason with you."

He tapped his temple. "In my head, I cannot reason with me, either."

"Okay, go on in there." Claire jerked her chin toward the door that separated the dining room from the kitchen. She wanted to hug him, kiss him on the forehead, but Alex wouldn't want that right now, so she held back. "I know she's waiting for you."

Alex pressed through the door without so much as a goodbye.

Claire swallowed hard as she leaned against one of the formal dining chairs and ran her fingers under her eyes in an attempt to clear any makeup smudges. Kendall and Brice were probably wondering where she was by now. More than likely she'd have missed calls on her cell. But she needed a moment to gain her composure. What were a few more minutes when she was already so late?

The sweet hints of cigar smoke hit her a second before her dad entered the room. He shook his head. "When are you going to get that child under control? How do you figure you can run a town if you can't even manage him?"

Awesome. So he'd overheard her failed talk with Alex.

She fiddled with her bracelets. Straightened them and then bunched them together again. "It's not as easy as that."

He stayed in the doorway. The house behind him was pure darkness. "I say it is."

She geared up to try and explain attachment disorder to him again, not that it would get him to finally grasp the concept that some people couldn't handle and control themselves at all times. "With what he—"

"Don't talk to me like I don't know anything about raising children. I raised you, didn't I?"

Technically, Mom had done the lion's share

of the child rearing in the Atwood home. For most of Claire's childhood her dad had been gone, traveling or locked away in his office until past midnight for days on end. As a child, Claire had lived to make him happy—to gain a glance, an ounce of his attention, if only momentarily. Dad had been good at giving the occasional head pat while he passed by, and that was about it.

Until the Evan situation. In that, her father had been nothing short of her hero. He'd arrived in time to pick up her broken pieces, set her on her feet again and guide her in the right direction. Without him, she probably would have tracked Evan down and pitifully thrown herself at his feet, begging him to love her. Thankfully, Dad had saved her from making a total fool out of herself. He had earned her respect that day and every day after with his patience when it came to her constantly going for another degree while dodging her parents' relentless urging for her to find someone worthwhile to marry.

He covered a phlegmy cough. "Well, didn't I?"

"Alex is different. His circumstances are different."

"Don't try to pawn off those lies the psychologist came up with. Quack doctors!" He spit the words as if they were curses. "They spin a garbage load of hogwash so that weak people can feel better about themselves. My pa tossed me out of the house when I was fourteen. He got remarried after my ma died, and his new wife wanted the kids out." He thumped his chest. "I don't have one of those fancy attachment disorders from that, now do I? I went out and made something of myself. Had my first million before my twenty-first birthday."

"I know your story, Daddy."

"Then tell that boy to shape up." He pointed at the door to the kitchen.

Arguing with Dad was as pointless as yelling into the wind. But his attitude had the potential of being damaging to Alex, so she tried to keep their contact to a minimum when she could. Most of the time Dad was busy working, so it wasn't all that hard to keep them separated.

Still, she liked to be aware of what Alex might have to face. "Are you planning on hanging out with them tonight?"

"Can't. I have work. A business doesn't run itself. Not a successful one."

"I know."

He took in her outfit as if for the first time. "You look too nice to go spend time with the likes of the Daniels gang. They'll all be there, the whole pitiful lot of them."

"I'm not going for the benefit of the Danielses. I'm going for Kendall. She's my friend. You know that. I'll support her no matter who she chooses to marry." And really, Evan's brother Brice seemed like the perfect fit for Claire's energetic and constantly optimistic friend. Brice's calm and steady demeanor balanced Kendall out, whereas she coaxed smile after smile from a man who not that long ago had been known as the town's grumpy hermit.

Claire had memories dating back to grade school of overhearing her father rail about the Daniels family. Mom always shrugged it off, saying there was bad blood between the families that Claire wouldn't be able to understand. True, because she was thirty now and she still didn't get it. Well, she understood why he wouldn't like Evan, but Brice had proved himself kind and devoted to Kendall. And that's really all she cared about where her friend's happiness was concerned.

Her father braced his hand on the door frame. "Kendall was an excellent business partner. I almost wished she would have stayed with me longer before paying back her loan so quickly."

Claire twisted the straps of her tote in her hands. "I really need to leave."

"I'd say have fun, but I don't think that's possible where you're going."

She slipped her heels on, gathered her bags and headed out. As she drove away from the gated Marina Lights subdivision she tried to lock away all thoughts of Alex's troubles and her father's less than kind attitude toward mental and emotional issues. But even when she was successful at doing that another worry roared like a caged cougar.

Evan would be at the dinner and at the wedding, filling the spot of best man. How could she manage her conflicting emotions about him when they had to walk down an aisle together? Under normal circumstances the situation would have been difficult for her, but this weekend marked what would have been the one-year anniversary of her and Auden's wedding.

Most of the time she was confident that breaking off her engagement had been the right decision, but sometimes...sometimes she wondered if she had blown her last shot at a future. Being so close to Evan—to the love she'd felt in the past, the one that had made her realize she wouldn't ever feel that way about Auden—hurt. It made the failure that marked her life fresh, tossing it in her face again and again. *This would have been your life. Except you weren't enough for him. In the end, Evan didn't want you.*

She would smile and laugh and pretend that proximity to him had no effect on her whatsoever. A total lie. Between Evan pulling her into his arms last weekend, his encouragement at the snow festival, the dependability he'd displayed while planning the Valentine's Day Shuffle and the way she kept catching him staring at her with his full-on intensity, her heart was in trouble. Despite knowing better—despite knowing that he was someone who had used her and abandoned her— she had instantly reacted to the shelter of his embrace. She'd have to work double time on almost depleted emotional reserves in order to protect her heart.

Evan Daniels was just as dangerous as ever.

Claire was running late.

The rest of the wedding party, along with Laura, Kendall's father, stepmother and half siblings, was gathered around a table at Agostini's Italian Restaurant. Kendall's siblings were as loud and outgoing as she was, and their conversation filled the private room to bursting. While everyone else wolfed down chicken Alfredo and made jokes about the amount of garlic Brice and Kendall were consuming, Evan kept his arm slung over the empty chair beside him, saving it for Claire.

Worry etched a deeper mark into Evan's usual calm each time Kendall tried to call her maid of honor and got only voice mail. Where could she be? What was the holdup?

She'd mentioned the rehearsal yesterday after her landslide win at the math contest. So it wasn't as if she'd forgotten. Something was keeping her away.

Evan pushed back from the table. "I'll run to her house. See if something's wrong."

Brice caught his eye. "You think that's a good idea?" He knew that Sesser had warned Evan to keep his distance from his property years ago.

"She's not answering my texts." Evan stood, slipping his phone into his back pocket.

Beside him, Laura gripped his wrist. "If something was wrong, she would have told you." She tugged, trying to get him to sit. "You're the first person she would have sent a message to."

"The roads are covered in black ice. Her car could be in a ditch. Who knows—"

Kendall untangled herself from Brice's side. "She's here!" The bride-to-be launched herself at Claire, pulling the slender woman into a bear hug.

Palpable relief seeped through Evan's shoulders and the muscles that crisscrossed his rib cage. A breath shuddered out. How was it that he'd gone years without worrying about her, but after a few weeks of contact he was a wreck over her well-being? Claire had mastered life in New York just fine. She was no longer the high school girl who'd asked him to put his hand at the small of her back when they entered a room. She was strong and capable and didn't need him anymore.

In truth, she never had.

Claire offered an apology to the group and flashed a smile to the room. Her gaze skirted over Evan before he could meet it. In the glow of the flickering candles that lined the tables, Claire looked flawless in a fitted, blue knee-length dress and heels. She and he were usually the same height, but whenever she put on heels she won by a couple inches. Stuff like that bothered some men, but it had never been an issue for Evan. She had a coat draped over her arm and a sparkling clip arranged in her hair. More important than all that, though, was the fact that her eyes were red and puffy.

Back when they were dating she'd had trouble making friends. Evan was glad that she and Kendall had bonded so quickly, but did Claire have anyone else to talk to? Despite all the years and tarnished memories between them, his heart went out to her. Besides, they'd come to a peaceful truce for the mayoral race.

It was okay to be concerned about a friend.

Especially one he was in love with.

As the rest of the group reclaimed their seats and dived into eating again, Evan pulled out the chair next to him and offered it to Claire. "Looks like you're stuck by me."

She laid her coat over the back of the chair and claimed her seat. A waiter rushed in with a hot plate and set it in front of her. Steam wafted over her. She picked up a fork, poked at the linguini and sighed.

Evan bumped his knee into hers and found her hand under the table, capturing it in his. "Why were you crying?"

Her eyes went wide. "How do you know—"

"I can tell." He kept his voice low and bent close so no one could overhear them.

She shook her head and a small, sad smile came onto her face. "You always could."

"You okay?" He pressed his knee into hers again; she pressed back.

"It's Alex. He had another outburst."

Evan's thumb traced a lazy circle over her palm. "Everyone okay?"

"Physically? Yes."

"I'm sorry it's difficult. He's worth it, though."

"Oh, I know. I love him." She closed her fingers around Evan's, her grip firm and determined. "He's my son, Ev. I just… I wish I could get through to him. I wish he understood that I will love him no matter what— that he doesn't have to do or be or become anything to keep my love. He doesn't comprehend that."

He doesn't have to do or be or become anything to keep my love.

The words were meant for Alex, but they pierced Evan's heart. How long had he striven to become someone worthy of the sacrifices Brice had made in order to protect him? He tried to make Brice happy—to do whatever he could so his brother would be proud. God, too, if Evan was being honest. He was involved in three different ministries in church and still felt as if he wasn't doing enough. There was a story in the Bible about someone dying and Jesus saying, "Well done, my good and faithful servant." It troubled Evan. He often thought that if he was standing in front of God he would be told, "You could have been so much more."

Evan cleared his throat. They were talking about Alex, not him. The focus should be on Claire's son and what could be done to help him. Evan was a grown man. If he couldn't figure out his life and if he still struggled to accept God's love, that was no one's problem but his.

"Give him time." He patted Claire's hand and finally released it. "I think there's a lot of adults who don't grasp that concept, either."

Chapter Ten

The wedding ceremony had been simple but beautiful, a perfect mixture of Brice's rugged side and Kendall's light and positive presence, and the reception proved to follow that theme. When Kendall first told Claire that she was going to hold her reception inside the barn at Crest Orchards, Claire had quickly advised her against it.

But she had been wrong.

She'd peeked into the reception venue from the small waiting area where the bridal party was holed up until they were announced. Ten circular tables lined the walls of the barn. They were decorated tastefully with white tablecloths, but the centerpieces were the stars of the show. It looked like someone had sliced through a tree trunk to get perfect segments of wood showing all the rings of the tree's life. On top of each sanded, polished slab was a pretty vase with artfully arranged flowers and a vintage picture frame with a table number. The tree detail was Evan's handiwork; Claire didn't have to ask to know that much. He'd always been talented at woodworking and he'd honed his craft over the past decade, turning it into pure art.

Perhaps tourists flocked to his furniture store every summer for more than just an eyeful of attractive man.

White fabric hung in loose billows from the exposed barn beams and white twinkle lights were strung above the fabric, giving a soft glow. At three separate points giant chandeliers dangled through the fabric, and someone had taken the time to weave flowers through their wooden frames.

The entire room oozed an understated elegance that made Claire's chest ache with longing for her own happy ending. But she had no hope of celebrating a day like this. Not after being abandoned at her first wedding and breaking off the engagement before reaching her second chance at being married. Kendall and Brice stood behind her in line as they waited to be announced by the deejay. Claire glanced back at the wrong moment.

Brice was nuzzling the side of Kendall's face. "How's your evening, Mrs. Daniels?"

Kendall turned toward her husband, trailed her fingertips along his jaw. "Best day of my life. Hands down."

"My goal is to get that answer from you every single day, for the rest of our lives." He laid a soft kiss on her cheek.

Kendall smiled and ran her hand down the front of his suit coat. "I'm up to the challenge if you are."

"No challenge, my dear wife. It'll be my pleasure." He sealed the promise with a kiss.

Claire ducked and turned back around, ashamed to have listened in on the couple's sweet moment for so long. Their exchange left her feeling hollow and raw.

She would never have what they did, would she?

A country song blasted through the speakers as Kendall's dad and stepmother were announced to the crowd. Cheers went up as they walked into the room and took their places at the head table. Next Kendall's adorable niece and nephew were announced as the ring bearer and flower girl. They rushed into the room together, leaving Claire next.

Where was Evan? She glanced around but didn't spot him.

The deejay launched into details about how everyone should stand and toast the bride and groom when they were announced. He said a few words about the wonderful couple and how he knew them both from a Bible study they attended. The middle-aged man launched into a story about how Brice and Kendall had encouraged him to pursue his wife and save his marriage. The imagery he painted was touching and it also bought time.

Claire pressed her palm to her chest and rubbed against the burn she felt. She would never know love, not again. When Evan hadn't shown at the courthouse he'd stolen every prospect of her ever experiencing her own happily-ever-after.

Because she had loved him. Completely. Entirely. She'd given him everything. More than she should have. But apparently, it hadn't mattered.

She could never feel that way about a man again. That strongly. Her parents didn't believe her, but she'd tried with Auden—really tried to fall for him. Auden Pierce had been perfect on paper. He was everything that made her parents proud, but she hadn't loved him. In the end, she hadn't felt for him close to a quarter of the affection she'd felt for

Evan. That's when she'd realized that it was no use dating anyone going forward.

If she could love a man who obviously didn't care for her—love him so much it hurt—then she couldn't trust herself. Not now, not ever. Her heart had proved to be just as much of a traitor as that man who had irrevocably wounded it.

Speaking of which… Evan was *still* nowhere to be seen.

The deejay's overenthused voice crackled on the speakers. "Next, let me introduce the best man and the maid of honor." Applause filtered through the thin wall between the large room in the barn where all the guests were seated and the alcove where Claire stood with Brice and Kendall. *Evan, if you don't show…* He'd left her here to walk into the reception area alone, hadn't he?

"Evan Daniels, dashing brother of the groom. And Claire Atwood, stunning best friend of the bride," the deejay announced.

Panic flipped around like a beached fish inside her stomach.

"Where's my brother?" Brice growled from behind her.

Claire lifted her chin and squared her shoulders. It wouldn't be the first wedding she'd walked into without him.

"I'm here. I'm here." Evan slipped between the bride and groom, a huge smile taking over his features. Why did he have to look so appealing? Like some hunky James Bond stand-in wearing a tux.

He swooped in, effortlessly wrapped his arm around Claire's waist and steered her into the room as if nothing was wrong. People cheered and smiled at them. A little old lady in a pink confection of a dress at one of the front tables gave Claire a thumbs-up and made a kiss face. Others clicked cameras or held their cell phones out for video as the two made their way to the head table.

Evan rotated between pumping his fist and waving at the guests as if he and Claire were riding on a parade float. His other arm kept her snug to his side so their hip bones pressed together. And she didn't mind the weight of his arm around her or the warmth of his hand at the small of her back. She *should* mind it.

She wanted to lash out at him for leaving her in the lurch until the last second, but at the same time, she didn't want him to remove his hand from her waist before he had to. It was too comforting. Too familiar. And they could get away with it here and no one would think anything. It was a wedding; they were best man and maid of honor—physical contact came with the job. And while she knew she shouldn't enjoy his attention…one night couldn't hurt.

Besides, after a full week of feeling wrung out by issues with Alex, conversations with her dad and thoughts about the impending, far-reaching desert that was her love life, she wouldn't turn down the confidence boost that accompanied Evan's attention. Even if it set her up to crash and burn tomorrow.

What was wrong with her?

Claire dug her elbow into his side and leaned close enough to breathe in his tantalizing cologne. So not helpful. "Where were you?"

He inclined his head and smirked at her. The glow from the twinkle lights made his green eyes glisten. "What kind of best man would I be if I didn't fancy up their getaway car a little?"

All the frustration she'd experienced a minute ago dissipated, like a balloon left untied. *Decorating the car, not ditching anyone.*

She allowed him to lead her around the back of the head table. He pulled out her chair.

"You're the worst," she muttered as she sat down.

"Aw, don't be mean." He helped her scoot her chair into place. With his hands still on the back of it he leaned so he could whisper in her ear, "You keep that up and I'll make sure all eyes are on us during the dance."

Her back went ramrod straight. "What dance?"

The deejay announced Brice and Kendall as Mr. and Mrs. Daniels, and the entire room went wild, cheering and clanking their cups as the couple entered.

No one watched Evan and Claire.

"That's right." He kept his head near hers, the roughness of his jaw catching strands of her hair. He wiped them away, dropped his hand to her shoulder and squatted beside her chair. "You were late to the rehearsal. After Brice and Kendall's first dance, we're supposed to join them on the floor."

Claire swiveled in her chair and delighted in the fact that the motion tossed him off balance. He dropped his hand from her shoulder and used it to catch himself from falling.

She rammed her finger into his chest. "Evan. Alfred. Daniels." She punctuated each of his names with another poke of her pointer finger. "You even *think* about embarrassing me out there and I'll make certain that your toes are so sore you can't walk tomorrow. And you have a 5k to run."

A playful smile tugged on his lips and he cocked his head. "Is that...a threat?"

"It's a promise."

Evan rose to his feet and performed a quick bow. "Until later, Miss Atwood."

"You're such a nerd," she called after him.

Kendall and Brice rounded the table to take their places between Evan's and Claire's seats. Claire's friend caught her eye and raised her eyebrow in a silent question, then jerked her chin toward Evan. The bride had badgered Claire with questions about what had happened between her and Kendall's now brother-in-law many times in the past nine months, but Claire had never budged beyond explaining that they had dated a long time ago.

What must she think after the last few weeks?

Claire offered a shrug, because what else could she do?

After the waiter collected their empty soup bowls Kendall leaned her elbow on the table and zeroed in on Evan. "So, wonderful new brother of mine, I have a question for you."

Evan picked up his goblet of ice water and chugged some. Chewed a piece of ice. Another. Why did tradition dictate that the bride sat between the groom and the best man, anyway? He should have been seated beside his brother, not Kendall. He liked Kendall fine, but she could be one determined spitfire when she wanted to be. And at the moment her laser focus was aimed squarely at him.

Besides, he had something he needed to tell Brice. At one point during the wedding ceremony, Evan had thought he'd spotted their younger brother, Andrew, at the back of the church. Funny thing about that was no one had heard from or seen Andrew in years. Was it seven now? Evan had lost count. Maybe his mind had been playing tricks on him. Either way, he felt that Brice should know.

He swallowed the last of the ice shards, pushed the image of Andrew away and gave Kendall all his attention. "I don't think I'm allowed to tell you no on your wedding day, so go ahead and ask."

She yanked on the long skirt of her dress and kicked her shoes off under the table. "You and Claire."

"That's not a question."

"I know you two dated."

"Still not a question."

"You two have been eyeing each other all day and were cozy at Agostini's last night.

And there's all those pictures of you two that *Goose Tales* keeps posting."

"Yet again, not a question."

Kendall let out a groan and shoved his shoulder. "What's going on between you two?"

So Claire had never told her the details? Interesting.

"Today?"

She nodded.

"Nothing." He yanked on the sleeves of his tux. "We're doing our duties. Making your day grand and all that."

The waiter placed a helping of chicken limone and mashed baby reds in front of him.

Someone at table seven started clanking a glass. Kendall held up a finger, letting him know the conversation wasn't over, and then turned and planted one on Brice. She turned back toward Evan, smoothed her hands over her dress and started talking again as if nothing had happened. "I don't buy that for a second."

Evan sank his fork into the potatoes. "Well, that's all that's for sale."

Kendall placed her napkin on her lap. "Something more happened than anyone is telling me. I've tried to get it out of your brother and he says it's not for him to share."

"That." Evan took a bite of the chicken and took his time chewing it before continuing. "And he doesn't know everything."

Kendall set her hand on his wrist, stopping his motions. "Claire is my best friend."

Evan let go of his fork; it clattered against his plate. He hung his head and took a deep breath. "Which means you wouldn't like me if you knew the truth."

"What happened? Please." She jiggled his arm. "Pretty please?"

Even though it was her wedding, Evan knew too well that she'd keep trying to corner him all night until he gave her something.

Where to start? What to tell? *Keep it short.* "We planned to run away from our families and get married the day after her eighteenth birthday."

Kendall's eyes grew into saucers. "That clearly didn't happen, though."

"I didn't show up at the courthouse. Claire waited and I never came. She thought she was getting married and instead she left that night for New York. Eleven years passed before she set foot in town again."

Color drained from Kendall's cheeks. "Why? How could you do that to her?"

The photographer interrupted them. "If you two could lean together."

Evan wrapped his arm around Kendall's shoulder.

"Smile, please!" The big attachment on the camera surged with light. "Thanks, perfect."

Evan removed his arm from around his sister-in-law. He ran his palms back and forth over the itchy fabric of the rented tux pants. "I told you you wouldn't like me."

"Oh, I still like you. You're family. I'll always have your back. And I'll always believe the best about you, even in this."

He stared at his chicken limone and watched the sauce pool on the edge of his plate. He swallowed once, twice, before saying, "Thank you."

"But I need you to be more careful with Claire." Kendall speared a piece of asparagus on her plate with more gusto than necessary. "I know you're just really friendly and outgoing, but most people read that as you leading women on. All I'm saying is don't lead Claire on."

"Listen." Evan poked at his chicken. "The election will be held in just over a week and Claire and I won't have any reason to interact anymore."

An ache spread through his chest. Until

the words had left his mouth, he hadn't processed that he would lose Claire again. And soon. If she won, she'd have no reason to talk to him. The mayor hardly needed to solicit advice from a woodworker. If he won, she wouldn't want to talk to him, especially after the truth came out. He and Brice were going to push for permits to build a new dock and take business away from her father. In the end, that was the entire reason Brice wanted him to win. It all came down to Sesser.

Claire wouldn't be okay with that.

"One of us will win and the other person will fade away."

Kendall's brow pinched. "When you put it that way, it sounds downright depressing."

"It's the only way I see this panning out. Claire and I…it's not possible for us to be friends without someone getting burned." When they did try to be friends, the people around them were determined to pull them apart. Brice questioned every interaction, and Evan knew Sesser was putting pressure on Claire. Now Kendall was telling him to stay away.

The deejay announced it was time for the bride and groom to have their first dance.

"Fine," Kendall whispered as she rose from

her seat and took Brice's hand. "Just, for her sake, try not to be so charming."

"Will do, sis." He shoved the mashed potatoes around on his plate, no longer hungry.

The fact that he'd coaxed a smile, laughter and some back and forth teasing out of Claire on the way to their seats had made his day. It had made him want to try to keep her smiling all night.

Perhaps that was the problem.

He had no right to want to be the reason she smiled.

When the deejay called for the wedding party to join the bride and groom on the dance floor, Claire gulped down her last sip of water and then slipped her hand into Evan's. He led her to the center of the floor and the song began. Something low and sweet and incredibly sappy. No doubt Kendall had selected the playlist.

Evan placed his palm at the small of Claire's back. A tentative lift of his lips hinted at a smile. "This okay?"

She rested her hand on his firm shoulder. "As long as you keep those toes off of mine, we're good."

A gentle laugh rumbled in his chest. "If it's

any comfort, I dance a little better these days than I used to."

He took his hand off her spine and spun her out and away from him, timed exactly with the swell of the music. Just as smoothly, he drew her back into his embrace. However, this time when his arm came around her she was closer to him, her temple only a few inches from his shoulder. They weren't simply doing a box step. Evan moved them around the floor. He even dipped her.

It would have been so easy to lay her head against his shoulder and close her eyes, lose herself in the sway of their bodies. Listen to his heartbeat—her favorite sound—like the old days. Where her fingers rested on his shoulder, it was impossible not to feel the strength of the man. His muscles had been trained and hardened by years of manual labor, of sweat and honest work. His occupation was his gym.

His chin grazed her head as he tilted to look at her face, and that little movement, the knowledge of how near his lips were to her forehead, made her throat go dry. Could he feel her heart pounding away against her rib cage? Like if it beat hard enough, it could break free and reach him—reach home.

Foolishness, Claire.

But Auden had never held her like this. Gently and carefully, as if she was something infinitely precious that needed to be cherished. Someone who deserved thoughtful attention.

The flash of a camera snapped her out of her musing. These were Evan's arms. An ex-boyfriend, a heartbreaker, the man she wanted to beat in an election. Not cozy up to.

Had Kendall chosen the extended version of the song? Claire couldn't trust herself to remain rational in Evan's arms much longer.

Regaining control over her wayward emotions, she leaned back a fraction. "When did you learn to dance?"

His eyes connected with hers, their green hue vivid in the light of the hanging lanterns. "Laura drafts me whenever she wants to practice a part in whatever play she's in at that moment. Lately she's been on a musical spree, which means I've had to learn my share of choreography. But let's keep that between us, okay?" He made a show of glancing around, pretending he cared if they were overheard. "Can't go ruining my tough-guy reputation."

"Please." Claire chuckled. "You're about as *tough-guy* as a marshmallow and everyone in town knows it."

"I'm not—wait, I am." He pouted. Apparently Laura wasn't the only member of the Daniels clan with a flair for dramatic acting. "A marshmallow, that is. I let the first graders beat me at Candyland after Sunday school last week."

Evan would make such a good father. Her heart flipped at the realization.

She swallowed and forced her face to remain neutral. "See?"

His hand on her back tiptoed up to touch her hair. "I can't stand it when they're all sad after losing."

"Marshmallow." Her voice was far more breathless than she was comfortable with.

"Which are delicious and universally adored."

Just like you, her treacherous heart screamed.

The song was finally replaced by an upbeat rhythm as the deejay welcomed all the wedding guests onto the floor.

Claire broke away from Evan. "I have to find Alex."

Evan nodded and headed back to his place at the head table. She noticed that a couple other women approached him during the reception, but he didn't participate in another slow dance the rest of the night. For that matter, neither did Claire. After remembering how wonderful it felt to be in Evan's arms again, no one else would have been able to compare.

Chapter Eleven

The morning of the Valentine's Day Shuffle was crisp and clear, the perfect day for a run.

However, not the perfect day to be surrounded by love. At least, not for Claire.

Perhaps the distraction presented by the fund-raising teamwork challenge was for the best. If not for the commitment, Claire might have moped today and spent far too much time in melancholy reflection.

She parked her car and made her way over to the booth near the gazebo on the square to see if there were any last-minute details that required her attention. Even though she wasn't going to participate in the 5k, she wore running pants and a fitted thermal top to keep up appearances and blend with the crowd.

Heart-shaped balloons were strung in an arch that would serve as the finish line. A jazz band supplied by Goose Harbor High School played crooner love songs near the bandshell. The bake sale ladies hawked frosted heart sugar cookies and chocolate-dipped strawberries.

"Your Valentine will love these."

Today would have been her and Auden's one-year anniversary, if she'd gone through with the wedding. She hadn't planned on that realization rocking her so much. Claire slipped on her sunglasses, hoping it would hide any lingering trace of the tears she'd shed on her drive over. She didn't mourn her relationship with Auden, just the possibility that it had presented.

And the finality that today seemed to epitomize. Alone. Again. Always.

Had her life become better since ending the engagement? She had Alex, a huge positive. But she still didn't have a career or a life or something to claim as her own. She still felt so lost and useless. That was why winning the position of mayor meant so much to her. It was something she could claim as an accomplishment. She could hang on to that title and say *I matter, you picked me, I belong.*

"Here's your racing bib. Number 78!" Shelby Beck handed Claire a paper with a number on it and four safety pins. "Do you want to run with one of our shelter dogs? A few are still available."

Shelby jutted her thumb over her shoulder in the direction of a penned-in area where ten dogs were standing, tails wagging. She and her fireman fiancé ran a dog rescue facility near the dunes. They'd volunteered to help organize everything on the day of the race in exchange for being allowed to bring some of their dogs for people to take along on the run and consider adopting.

"Oh, I'm not running in the 5k. Just an organizer." Claire attempted to hand her number back.

Shelby skewed up her lips. "Says here you're registered as a runner. Paid and everything."

"It's a mistake. I didn't register."

"I did." Evan appeared at her side. "She's running."

Shelby laughed and handed over his racing bib. "This is between you two and I'm not about to get in the middle."

Claire stomped after Evan.

He hiked his leg, stepping into the fenced-in area. The moment he was in the enclosure the dogs surrounded him, sniffing, some with full-body wags.

"Which one?" Evan gave them each a head

scratch. He got down on one knee to consider a dog that looked like it might be a cross between a husky and a boxer. "I'm thinking this guy." The dog offered him a chin lick as he checked the animal's tag. "Er, girl. Says her name's Stella. Well, Stella, wanna run with us?"

"With him."

"Us." He clipped a leash onto the dog's collar and led her out of the enclosure. "The purpose of athletic wear isn't to prance around looking cute." His grin took on a wolfish quality. "Although, if it was, you'd have that covered." The second the words were out his smile froze. "I probably shouldn't have said that. Correction, I definitely shouldn't have said that."

With her sunglasses on, he couldn't tell if she was looking at him or not. Might not be able to assess if the heat blazing across her cheeks, which had no doubt colored them pink, meant she was upset or amused.

She let him squirm for another second. Then said, "It's fine. Except I definitely don't prance."

"Prove it by running."

Mr. Banks climbed up the steps of the gazebo and announced that the countdown for the race was about to begin.

Evan scooted past Claire, Stella happily bounding beside him. "What? Afraid you can't keep up?" he called over his shoulder.

Sometimes a good run cleared her mind. Participating in the Valentine's Day Shuffle while she was struggling with the significance of the day might actually be a good idea. At the least it would serve as a distraction for the next thirty or forty minutes.

Claire groaned, opened the safety pins and started affixing her number to the front of her shirt for timing purposes. Her parents kept a functioning workout room in their basement and Claire made good use of the treadmill. She'd never run a 5k outside, but how difficult could it be? There were people significantly older and younger than her lining up at the starting point. If they could do it, it shouldn't be an issue for her.

A horn blast signaled the start of the race and everyone surged forward. A lady jogging behind a double stroller wiped past her. Skylar Ashby ran beside her father, a white T-shirt pulled over her sweatshirt. In uneven, puffy paint letters across the back was the message Vote for Dad!

Claire kicked into high gear to catch up with Evan and Stella. This wasn't a formal part of the mayoral competition, but the people of Goose Harbor would treat it that way.

"Pace yourself," Evan warned when she came up beside him. The elements had turned his cheeks and the tip of his nose red.

Mile one wasn't so bad. But mile two? Oh, her lungs burned, her legs ached and talking was next to impossible.

Evan stayed beside her even though Claire could tell he could run much faster and was holding himself back. At least his breath was coming out in loud, jagged puffs. "Need to walk?"

She nodded, swallowed, licked her lips and stopped. Gulping air, she braced her hands on her thighs. Stella plopped down on top of Claire's shoes and looked up at her with sky blue eyes. She whined once, whined again. Hopped up and licked Claire's chin. Claire didn't have the strength to fight off the loving assault.

"Don't stop completely." Evan put his arm to her back and propelled her forward. "Once you stop, it's ten times as tough to keep going."

"This is so much harder than the treadmill." She panted, plodding onward. "Why is it so much harder?"

"You're pushing yourself forward, instead

of the machine doing it for you. The cold air doesn't help, either."

She bobbed her chin, breathing heavily. "And my feet still hurt from the heels I wore for the wedding. So not fair. You didn't have to wear heels."

He shoulder bumped her. "I wouldn't look as good in them as you did."

"A small comfort."

"Come on, let's try to jog." He started going faster and got in front of her. Stella barked as she vaulted to join him, clearly happy at the increased speed. "Mrs. Clarkson and her crew are power walking this thing and I don't want them to catch up to us."

At the final mile marker Evan reached for Claire's arm. "We're almost done now. Let's pick it up."

"Evan, I can't."

"You know they're going to be snapping pictures of us."

She moaned. "Tell me again, why did you talk me into doing this?"

"Because I know you're capable of more than you think you are."

She had no quick quip to throw back at him. No jest or flash of wit. Evan had faith in her, from silly things like running a 5k to believing she had it in her to succeed at following her dreams. That's why he'd encouraged her to paint the other day. He knew that was important to her. Knew that no one else cared about that long hidden desire of her heart.

With Evan in her life, she was stronger. Just being around him made her believe she was capable of scaling mountains, too. She rose to his challenges, but never felt like he'd be disappointed if she didn't reach them…only if she refused to try.

Over the past few weeks he'd proved that he was patient, kind, humble and self-sacrificing. He cared about protecting others and always hoped for the best.

Evan would make a far better mayor than Claire ever would.

Evan checked the dirty clothes hamper in Laura's room before starting the washing machine, then wiped down the vanity in the upstairs bathroom. Stella's nails clicked on the wooden floor as she shadowed him all over the house.

"Lie down and relax. You're home. It's all safe, Stella-bell." She pressed her head against his leg as he scratched behind her ear.

Shelby and Joel had given him enough pet food to make it through the weekend, but come Monday he'd head to a pet supply store and gather the items needed to take care of his new friend, including a nail trimmer. It wasn't as if he'd planned on bringing a dog home, but after their run together he couldn't hand her back. Stella was a sweetheart.

Anyway, Laura was seventeen and would be going to college soon enough. Now that he had grown accustomed to having someone else in the house he didn't want to face going back to being alone again.

Evan performed a cursory sweep of the basement area, because Laura and her friends were forever leaving an array of dishes and cups down there. His basement was fully refinished, complete with an air hockey table, foosball table, a few old-school arcade games and plenty of hangout space. Laura referred to the basement as her "domain" and had already informed him that she'd signed him up to host the cast party for the musical after the last show. Thankfully, that wasn't happening until March.

With the teamwork challenge out of the way, he could focus on the lesson plan for Sunday school tomorrow.

Mr. Banks had called Evan with the final fund-raising total. All of the close to $4,200 raised would go to the local organization Food for All. The food bank served the Goose

Harbor area and hosted a program that offered daily hot meals to children from low income families.

He had even shared a laugh with curmudgeonly Mr. Banks over the doughnut eating competition. Evan had signed up for a slot, but Claire had been right; after running, he had a hard time putting up a good fight. Caleb Beck won by a mere two bites, beating a couple of the police officers, including Caleb's best friend, Miles.

All in all, it had been a fun day. Well, other than the fact that Claire had seemed…distracted. Was that the correct word? She'd joked with him, but he'd had to drag the good humor out of her. Something was on her mind. More than likely, the upcoming completion of the mayoral race. It came down to what he'd discussed with Kendall yesterday at her wedding—his and Claire's truce was drawing to a close. After the vote, they'd go back to how it had been a month ago. Acting like the other didn't exist.

He didn't know how he was going to deal with that.

Evan headed to the kitchen to stow away his piles of junk mail and load the dishwasher. His doorbell rang. It was past seven on a Saturday night. Brice and Kendall were gone on their honeymoon and Laura's practice ran until nine. He lived in the middle of nowhere on a wide swath of land. But what if it was Andrew? He still believed he'd spotted their missing brother at Brice's ceremony.

He wiped his hands on the nearest dish-cloth, then went and opened the door.

Claire Atwood was in tears on his front porch.

His heart twisted. "What's wrong?" He reached for her, wanting to draw her out of the cold and maybe, if she was willing, into his arms to comfort her.

"Don't. Please." She hiccuped. Held up her hands to block him. "Just let me get this out without any interruptions."

The headlights of her car blazed in twin horizontal beacons at the bottom of his steps. The beams highlighted wispy snow flurry-ing in haphazard angles. Her engine was still running, the wipers sounding an intermittent click into the dark air. Instrumental music floated out of the open driver's side door.

"Claire, you're freaking me out." His pulse kicked into high gear as he took in the scene and her pained expression. "Is Alex okay? What's going on?"

"Please." She sniffled. "I just want to say something and leave."

"Okay." Evan braced his hands on either side of his entryway. If he didn't, he was certain he'd reach for her again, and that didn't seem to be helping matters. "Go ahead."

"If I had married Auden, today would have marked our one-year anniversary."

She was crying over Auden? Any hopes Evan had secretly harbored of trying to keep up a friendship with Claire after the election took a quick nosedive. If she was still pining for Pierce, he couldn't handle that.

Still, she'd come to him. If she wanted to confide in him about another man, he'd let her. He owed her that much. "Claire—"

"This is hard enough to say without interruptions." Her voice wavered, as did her body. She leaned and gripped the railing. "I've been thinking about it all day—praying about it. And I'm relieved, Evan. In the end I only feel relief, because I had no business marrying him. I didn't love him. Not like—" She closed her eyes tightly, shook her head. "It would have been a disservice to both of us."

And now he wasn't following. If she was relieved, why was she crying about their would-have-been anniversary? Evan opened his mouth to ask a question.

Claire held up her hand. "I'm not finished." She sucked in a deep breath and continued,

"You backed out on our wedding and I held that against you for a long time. I couldn't see before. I couldn't understand until I was in the same position."

"Claire. No." He dropped his hold on the door frame and stepped onto the porch. Stella's nails clicked beside him.

Claire spoke over him as she backed down the stairs. "I don't hold it against you anymore. I... I finally get it. I get why you did it."

He took a few more steps, ice nipping at the soles of his feet. Why didn't he ever wear shoes and socks in his house? "Stop."

She'd reached the front of her car. "I hope you find love, because you deserve every happiness in life. You're a good guy. The best guy."

Evan's feet cried for mercy when he reached the stairs. Stella whined, her head wiping between the two. "You can't say something like that and then not let me talk. Come inside. Please. Come talk to me."

"I'm sorry. I can't—" Her hand covered a sob. "I have to... I have to go."

"Claire, hold up—"

Stella barked happily, lurching after Claire. Evan caught the dog's collar, but the force of her unexpected movement dragged him down into the snow, giving Claire the seconds needed to get into her car and set it into Reverse. He bashed his knee on one of the porch steps on the way down.

"Claire. Wait!" She couldn't drop that on him and leave without giving him an opportunity to say something. "Claire!"

Her car backed down his driveway.

Hauling himself to his feet, Evan dragged Stella back inside and shoved his feet into the nearest pair of shoes. He fisted his keys on the way out and closed the door. Finding a coat or gloves would have taken too long.

He took a heartbeat to scan the area. She'd turned left out of his driveway. He owned the property all along the highway on that stretch and the road meandered, following a stream. Evan took off at a sprint, tearing through the forested part of his property. Dampness seeped into his tennis shoes, and his sockless heels rubbed raw with every step. Bare winter branches slashed at his legs, arms and chest, but he ignored their stings and ran harder. He had to make it to the curve by the stop sign before she did.

Give me speed, Lord. Help me.

His calves and thighs burned. Between the wedding yesterday and the race this morning, his muscles were begging for respite.

Not yet.

Evan pumped his arms and slid down an embankment, almost tumbling over himself. He no longer cared if they had tomorrow or not. Or if Brice would be upset. Or how it would affect his chance at office. He'd apologize to Kendall for breaking his word, but he wouldn't stay away from Claire any longer.

No sooner had he hobbled out of the woods than her car came around the bend. As she slowed to comply with the sign, he skidded onto the road, his palms to her hood as he rounded her car. They made eye contact through her windshield. Tears coursed down her cheeks and her mouth formed an O.

She started to open her door and step out. "Are you crazy? You could have—"

Evan stalked toward Claire, grabbed her around the waist and pulled her to him. His lips claimed hers in a fierce kiss and she answered in kind. He pushed a hand into her hair, knocking her hat onto the top of the car, and drew her body closer with his other hand pressed at the small of her back. He poured twelve years of missing her into the kiss, before finally parting.

Gasping for breath, he didn't know if his sprint through the woods had caused his lungs to feel as if they were going to burst, or if it was Claire. Probably Claire. It had always been her, hadn't it? His chest heaved. Claire pulled him in for a hug and he buried his face against her neck, inhaling the flowery scent that was her.

She shivered in his arms. Cuddling out in the frigid air was not the best course of action. He stepped back.

Her hand rose to her lips. "You don't have a coat. You have to be freezing."

"Believe me, I'm not. Not after that." He used a thumb to lift her chin. "Claire-bear, look at me." He drank in her watery gaze. "I appreciate what you said back there, but I had to catch you. You don't *get it*."

"But I do." She fisted a hand into the excess fabric of his shirt. "It makes sense now."

"No, you don't." He traced his knuckles along her jawline. Savoring the feel of her soft skin, he slipped his fingers into the red hair he often dreamed about. "And don't ever tell me you want me to fall for someone else, because it's not going to happen." He braced a hand against the roof of the car on either side of her. Leaned closer. "I loved you, Claire. That day I backed out—the biggest regret of my life is letting you go. I don't want to love someone else—I can't—because I still love you. I think I always will."

She inhaled sharply. "I'm so confused." Her hands slid down his chest. "None of this is computing."

"Let me explain everything." Maybe once he told her about Sesser's involvement…they could move on. Despite all the people who didn't want them to be together, and years of hurt and questioning, was it possible there was a future for them?

"I have to pick Alex up from Scouts. I'm already late." She glanced down at her driver's seat. "I—"

"We'll talk. This week. I'm not going anywhere." He let his hands fall away from her. As much as he wanted to beg her to stay and have a long conversation, she was a mother and needed to be there for her son. Evan wanted to support her in that. The snow was picking up and Alex would worry if she was late.

Evan pressed a soft kiss to her forehead. "Tomorrow?"

She clutched his shirt again and tugged him nearer, closing the small gap between them so she could rest her forehead against his collarbone. "Get in the car. Come with me."

"Are you sure?" He wanted to but… "We

can't exactly have that conversation in front of Alex."

"I just want you nearby…for a little while longer."

He nuzzled his chin into her hair. "All right, let's go pick up your son."

Chapter Twelve

Her tires fought for traction as she took the next corner at a crawl.

"The roads are slick." Claire's fingers were going white from holding the steering wheel so tightly.

"Go slow." Evan's voice was calm and even. Ever a rock, no matter what was happening. "I'm sure whoever's running Alex's meeting will realize about the storm. You're probably not the only parent delayed."

"The house is a minute or two over the town's border, past the abandoned summer camp, into Shadowbend."

"Good thing you came my way. My house is a lot closer to that than your parents'." He held his hands in front of the heat vents. They passed the old entrance to the former camp. "It looks... Are there lights on in there?"

The road curved before she could catch a glimpse.

While she and Evan were outside at the stop sign the snowfall had significantly increased. Five minutes later, they were inching into the winds of a blizzard. She hadn't noticed how bad the storm had become until they'd climbed into her car and buckled up. That was the problem—when she was around Evan everything else disappeared, including the controlled, logical reasoning she prided herself on.

Was that a good thing or a bad thing?

After she began driving, he'd fiddled with the temperature controls and then huddled in the passenger seat. Without a coat on, he had to be numb. Thankfully, he didn't broach the topic of *them*, so she could focus her complete attention on the treacherous roadway. Bless him for his restraint. Evan's personality could be categorized as impulsive, so if he wasn't talking when she knew he wanted to, he was doing it for her.

Her wipers beat a warpath at their top speed across her windshield, and still she was having a hard time making out the road.

Now that the adrenaline rush from their sudden kiss had worn off, Claire fought the pull of embarrassment. She'd begged him to come with her. Not to end the evening yet. Was she so in need of feeling wanted that she'd pull a man into her car? Put that way, she was pathetic. They would pick up Alex and then what?

But Evan had said he loved her.

What would she do with that statement? Could Evan truly be in love with her again? Moreover, did she want him to feel that way? Perhaps he didn't understand his own feelings. Maybe they were both simply attracted to each other, which was fine and well, but that wasn't love.

Except…she knew she loved him.

Sure enough, when they reached the house in Shadowbend there were four other vehicles picking up Scouts. Evan stayed at the car and promised to battle the buildup of snow on the front and back windows while she went in to retrieve Alex. Something so simple, being able to leave the car running on a cold day, but it twisted Claire's heart. Parenting was easier with two people.

Inside, Alex handed her a bag and then worked his arms into his heavy coat, performing a shimmy. "Your mom called. No power at the house. She went to a hotel." He zipped his coat and finally regarded Claire with a quirked eyebrow. "She said you should be better about picking up your phone. She sounded steamy."

Claire dropped to her knees to help him step into his boots. "*Upset* is a better word to use than *steamy*."

"Steamy means more what I want to say. Steam out of her ears." He moved his fingers to simulate smoke.

She ushered him out to the car and they told Evan about her mom's call.

Evan pivoted to address Alex in the back. "Wanna meet my dog?"

Alex swung his legs so his feet beat a tapping rhythm against Evan's seat back. "Since when do you have a dog?"

"Since today." Evan grinned with schoolboy excitement. "She's brown and white like a boxer, but has these blue eyes, and her ears stand up like a husky's. Long tail."

"Sounds cool. I want a dog." Alex sighed. He folded his arms and glanced toward Claire's seat. "But *she* says not in her dad's house." The boy perked up. "Did you know a dog's nose is ten thousand times more powerful than ours?"

"I love that you know that without looking

it up." Evan beamed with something akin to fatherly pride. "You're like a walking smart-phone."

Claire set the car into Drive. "Evan, we can't impose."

"Sure you can." He gave a thumbs-up to Alex as he turned back to face the front. "My house is closest. And if the power's out in the Marina Lights subdivision, those people have probably already swarmed the hotels and snatched up every available room. It's Valentine's Day weekend, so I can't imagine there were that many rooms left to begin with. Laura's home," he added. "I called her while you were inside."

"Fine." Claire flipped on her turn signal in the direction that would take them back to Evan's. "But only until the storm lets up."

The storm didn't let up.

Evan headed upstairs to put fresh sheets on his bed and make sure the guest bedroom had everything it needed, while Claire stayed with Alex and Laura, who were playing with Stella. Fortunately, he'd been accused of being a neat freak and the charge was true, so his room and the bathroom were already clean and ready for guest use.

The second his feet hit the stairs Stella bolted to the bottom and yelped, waiting for him.

Laura smiled up at him. "You sure won her heart quickly. What'd you do? Slip her doggy treats all day?"

Claire had her back to them as she rinsed a few cups in the sink. "He has that effect on a lot of women." She spoke softly, probably meaning to say it under her breath, but they all heard.

Laura pointed at Claire's back. She mouthed *You and her?* and waggled her eyebrows, emphasizing her point. The memory of yanking Claire into his arms and kissing her soundly made keeping eye contact with his sister difficult.

"You're blushing!" Laura stage-whispered, and did a little hop.

Thankfully, the whole exchange went over Alex's head, as he hugged Stella's neck. "She's so good. Did you know a group of huskies once saved a town full of sick kids? It was in Alaska. There's a movie about it. It made me like them a lot. I wish she was my dog."

Stella spared him a lick down the side of his face and then went back to anxious prancing as she waited for Evan to reach the bottom of the stairs.

"Bedrooms are ready. Alex." Evan pointed. "Guest bedroom is the first door in the hallway on the right. Bathroom's across from it. There's an unopened pack of toothbrushes on the counter, so pick one and leave one for your mom. Claire, my room's set for you. It's—"

"I'll sleep on the couch." Claire didn't turn around, but he saw her fingers dig into the edge of the countertop.

Laura dropped her hand onto Alex's head and ruffled his almost-black hair. "Hey, buddy, let me give you a tour of upstairs. I'll even show you where Evan keeps a secret stash of old comic books."

Evan winked a thank-you to his sister as they pounded up the steps past him. He patted Stella's head and continued into the kitchen. "Claire."

"There's no reason for you to be kicked out of your room on my account."

"I fall asleep on the couch three or four times a week because I get sucked into watching some late night nature documentary. Or I'm working in the garage and by the time I realize it's late I'm too tired to haul myself upstairs. Ask Laura. She'll tell you, me and this couch are old friends."

"But it's *your* room."

"Don't make a big deal about this. It's a bed with clean sheets and you're snowed in. No different than a hotel, except for the no room service part."

She rolled her eyes. "You're impossible."

"I'm not having a guest sleep on the couch when there's a bed available. I'll stay down here, use the bathroom down here, and you can be up there with the kids. It's the best given the situation."

"Fine."

"Mom!" Alex hollered from somewhere upstairs. "Do you want the green toothbrush or the one I dropped on the ground?"

Evan couldn't help but laugh. "Oh, man. Choices."

She shook her head, a sad smile playing across her lips. "I had thought we would talk, about everything…but now, with Alex… Us, together here, overnight…" She wrung her hands. "I'm a mom, Evan. He's still trying to accept everything. I don't—"

Evan bowed his head and prayed he'd say the right thing. "Alex is your top priority, as he should be. We'll figure it out, I promise. He needs you. Go. Don't worry about me."

* * *

Hours later Evan stared at the ceiling, watching branch shadows cast by his porch lamps move in the wind. Old trees had popped and groaned all around the house during the storm and he hadn't been able to sleep, worried that one of them would fall. A hazard of living in the middle of a forest. But the storm had stilled within the last thirty minutes.

At least the one outside. The one in his heart? Not so much.

He'd meant what he said to Claire, that it was more important for her to take care of Alex than to have an overdue relationship conversation with him. Still, he'd held out hope that she'd come back downstairs after tucking Alex into bed.

He swung his feet to the floor and sat up. Elbows on his knees, Evan scrubbed his hands over his face. If sleep was going to elude him, he might as well go out and clear as much of the snow as he could. Their church service started early and he was supposed to be there well before the service began to help with setup. Besides, if the roads were clear, then Claire and Alex would have to leave straight from breakfast so they could head home and change and still get to church in time. Shoveling while he thought accomplished more than staying in bed.

Stella bounded outside with him. She ran in ecstatic doggy zigzags, nipping at the snow and then hopping back to bark at it.

"Stella-bell, hush. People are sleeping."

Properly subdued, she took to rolling in every shovelful of snow he heaved off the driveway, making the process take three times longer than usual. Actually, the whole chore could have been done in fifteen or twenty minutes if he'd opened his shed and taken out his riding mower. It had a shovel attachment, which was how he usually cleared the drive. But not at midnight when people were sleeping inside.

Stella spotted motion on the front porch before he noticed, and took off sprinting to see who had joined them outside.

Claire placed two mugs on the steps and then spread a flannel blanket out on the porch. She sat down. "Break time."

Evan stomped the snow off of his boots and headed over to her. "I didn't wake you, did I?"

She shook her head and handed him a steaming mug. "I couldn't sleep."

"Me, either." He sat down beside her and took a sip. Hot chocolate exactly the way he loved it. She'd discovered his stockpile of peanut butter cups.

"You always were a hard worker, throwing yourself fully into whatever you put your mind to. I admired that about you." She gestured with her mug, indicating the headway he'd made on the driveway. "After everything, that might be what hurt the most. When you commit, you're all in. But when it came to me, I didn't inspire that in you."

"That wasn't it at all." He set his hot cocoa down on the step beside him and took her free hand in both of his. "I don't know where to start or how to say it without—"

"Just say it. It's time."

He had a hard road ahead of him. Claire knew that her father wasn't the best person, but he was still her family. Evan didn't want to paint Sesser as a monster. Then again, he could hardly make light of him blackmailing an eighteen-year-old.

"On the way to our wedding I stopped to buy you flowers. Peonies."

"My favorite."

"We were getting married at a courthouse." He shrugged. "You were having to do without so many of the normal things girls want on their wedding day. I at least wanted you to have a bouquet. Anyway, your dad must have been following me. He blocked my car in the parking spot and refused to move his own until I talked to him."

She opened her mouth. In shock? Or to say something? But nothing came out, so he kept going. Might as well press on with the story while she was willing to listen.

"He cornered me. There were two other guys in his car. Big guys." Men who had sneered and cracked their knuckles as they flanked Sesser. "It was like a scene out of a mob movie."

"I had no idea." Claire set down her mug and used the hand he wasn't holding to swipe at her eyes. "My dad?"

Evan fought the desire to forgo the story in favor of drawing her against his chest again. Telling her he was here now and was never going to leave.

He cleared his throat. "He had this file with him. It was full of bank statements and collection notices. They were all in Brice's name. Sesser told me that my dad had racked up a ton of loans in my brother's name and Sesser owned a lot of them. If he called in the debts, it would ruin Brice's life. Brice was in college at the time—he had no clue. He was working so hard to make something of himself outside of our family."

Her fingers tightened around his. "Ev." She spoke his name in the same way she would say "sorry."

"Then he told me that if I didn't walk away from you, he'd use his connections to have Brice expelled from university. He also promised to make it impossible for Brice to ever find a welcome at any school in the state. I believed he was powerful enough to make good on that threat."

Claire was thoughtful for a moment before she nodded. "He was. Still is."

"If I didn't show, if I left you, he vowed to make the debts go away, leave my parents alone for good and see that Brice's schooling would be anonymously paid for in full."

"I see." Ice edged her voice.

Evan swallowed hard. He thought she'd been following the logic, understanding. He had to make her see that, given the situation, he'd done the only thing he could. "I owe Brice my life, Claire. You know that more than anyone."

"So that's all it took?" She jerked her hand from his. Crossed her arms over her chest and turned her knees so they were no longer bumped up against his. "Some of my dad's money?"

Her words hit Evan with the force of a slap. "You make it sound like a payoff."

Claire arched an eyebrow. "Wasn't it?"

Stella crawled up the steps and curled against his side. Picking up on the tension, she let out a whine as she set her head on his thigh.

If he'd pushed back at Sesser, her father would have found another way. They were young, and even if they'd run far away from Goose Harbor, his influence was far-reaching. "Did I really have a choice?"

"Yes. You could have come to me that day and told me everything. We could have faced my dad together. We could have gone to the police to get my father's threats on file."

"Do you honestly believe that at eighteen we could have stood up to your dad?"

"I guess we'll never know, will we? I used to believe we could face anything together." Her voice cracked and she turned to look out at the fresh snow blanketing the side yard.

He caught her hand, willing her to warm to him again. "It was the single hardest thing I've ever done in my life. His bodyguards tossed me into the back of a second car. He drove to the courthouse and they made me watch as you cried on the steps. Sesser came to where they had me at the back window, showed me plane tickets and told me your stuff was already packed. You never told me you'd applied to Columbia. I had no clue you were registered to start there in the fall. If we'd married that day, I would have been responsible for holding you back."

"That was my choice to make!"

"You should have told me. That whole time, you had a backup plan." He kept his voice gentle. "Once I saw the acceptance letter, I realized that you were meant for far better things than marrying a woodcarver with no aspirations outside of this town. I never would have been good enough for someone like you."

Evan pictured his mother. She'd always been a tiny woman, but as she aged and bitterness wore on her, she'd wasted away to sharp edges and scowls. Sheryl Daniels had married his father when she was already pregnant with Brice, and she held the mistake over Brice's head with anger even now. Their mother was quick to say something spiteful, especially toward their father, but Evan had to believe that they had loved each other at some point, long ago. And he never wanted that...never wanted to love a woman and then have her later regret being shackled to him.

If you leave this car and marry her, you're selfish. Full-on selfish. You'll take away every opportunity she has in this life. You don't deserve someone like her. My daughter is smart and capable, but if you do this, you'll destroy her and that's not love, son. If you love her, like you supposedly say you do, then you'll let these men drive you away and I'll never have to deal with you again. Understood?

Her next question surprised him. "Does Brice know?"

Evan had thought—hoped—she might argue about him not being worthy of her. Apparently, though, she agreed.

He shook his head. "None of it."

"You have to tell him. He deserves to know."

They were silent for a long time.

Claire rolled her shoulders. She warred between two reactions. She wanted to throw her arms around Evan, tell him she understood and wanted to start fresh with him, that she loved him. But equally, she wanted to yell at him. The mystery of Evan's abandonment had been solved, but the answer left her feeling more alone than before. Because everything came down to a single point—when given the option, he hadn't chosen her.

Brice was more important. Her father's dreams about her future were more important. Evan's need to belittle himself was more important. Deep down, he must not have believed their love was strong enough to weather those storms.

But Claire had. She'd rushed off to school only to bandage her broken heart. She would have gladly chosen a life with Evan over her degrees and experiences.

She rolled her shoulders again. "If this is all true, then why didn't you answer any of my letters?"

"I didn't— You wrote to me?" Evan jerked his head back. His surprise was genuine.

"I sent them to your parents' house." It was the only address she had.

"I never went back there, after that day." He braced his hand on the porch behind him and leaned back. "I moved into the apartment over Mrs. Clarkson's garage. My parents… If you wrote I never got them." He rubbed his hand over the top of his stocking hat. "Both of my parents have something against your family. They must have tossed them." He shook his head. "I gave your mom letters, too. I'm guessing they never made it to you, either?"

Her mother had prevented their relationship, as well? Betrayal sliced deeper into Claire's heart. She'd known what her father was capable of but hadn't imagined her mother playing a part.

Evan was still waiting for an answer, but words cost too much at the moment, so she shook her head.

"When I never heard from you, I took that as confirmation that what I did was for the best. That you didn't love me." He scrubbed his hand around his jaw. "I figured you hated me."

He was determined to see everything in that light—to believe he didn't deserve to be happy and loved. Wasn't he? Telling him he was wrong wouldn't solve that. Evan would have to realize his worth on his own. No woman could give him that.

They didn't need to dwell on the past and what-ifs any longer. The conversation had happened, answers had been given and it was time to move on with both their lives.

Getting ready to stand, she dusted off her pant legs. "Aren't we a sad pair? Both jumping to any available conclusion."

"Claire...if we'd married, you probably wouldn't have Alex."

"Is that your way of saying it was all God's plan?" Was he suggesting that God had wanted her to cry herself to sleep for months on end? To waste time with Auden?

To feel lost and alone for twelve years? *That* was God's plan for her life?

"I was thinking more along the lines of, isn't it amazing that God uses our failings to still do good. When we make a mess of things—when *I* make a mess of things—He doesn't stop working or being faithful."

Alex—he was the positive out of all that had occurred. She'd had the same thought before. Adopting her son *was* worth all the pain she'd been through in the past, but was it too much to hope that the future could be different? Brighter?

"I don't hate you," Claire said. "I could never hate you." Her shoulder touched his and she let it stay there. Contact. It wasn't so bad. "Don't you wish life could be like this snow?"

"What do you mean?"

"Look at it. It's perfect. Unspoiled. If only we could figure out how to pull a proverbial blanket of snow over all that's happened between us… I want to believe there's a way, still."

God, I love this man, but I'm also really hurt by all that's happened between us. Is that wrong? Can this still happen?

Evan tilted his head. "The snow doesn't make things perfect. It's only hiding the problems and ugly parts of my yard. It may look pristine, but over there—" he pointed to some trees "—I never got around to removing the leaves from that part of the yard. They're a slimy, rotting pile. You can't see them, but they're there. A facade, as pretty as it can be, is never better than the mess of reality."

Then he pointed beyond her car. "On that side of the driveway I have a mud pit that refuses to grow grass. It's unsightly in the spring. The snow may cover those problems, but they're all still there and still need to be dealt with. Issues don't go away simply because they're covered or ignored."

She sighed and let her head rest on his shoulder. She was tired, from today, yes, but it more had to do with a tiredness in her soul. Right now, for a few minutes, she wanted to be close to Evan and not worry about what that meant. "You just turned that snowfall into something *way* bigger."

He brought his arm around her back. "I might have gotten a tad carried away."

"Just a tad. But joking aside, it's a good way to look at things."

"So…if we're choosing *not* to ignore hard things, where does that leave us?"

And that quickly, reality came crashing in. Claire lifted her head off his shoulder and closed her eyes, taking in a long breath of air and then blowing it out. "It leaves us with an election next weekend. Let's finish this race, and after that, we'll talk."

"After the election." He got to his feet and offered her a hand up. "I can live with that."

Chapter Thirteen

It was late on Wednesday night. Claire's hands were shaking.

Please don't take my dad. Not yet. He doesn't know You.

Thankfully, Mom had called 911 before barging into Claire's apartment to tell her through broken sobs that Dad had collapsed in the dining room and was unresponsive. Every first aid video Claire had ever watched had flooded into her mind. She'd started chest compressions without knowing if she was doing them correctly, but the paramedics had assured her she had done everything she could. Mom had gone along in the ambulance.

Claire focused on the phone in her hand and on Mom's anxious voice on the other end. "The doctor is saying he may not make it.

They rushed him inside and tossed around the words *heart attack*. I can't be here alone. I need you, Claire."

"Mom, Alex is sleeping. He has school tomorrow."

"Can't you wake him up and bring him with you? This is his *grandfather*."

"Let me see what I can do. Okay? Calm down, Mom. Take some deep breaths. I'll call you back in a few minutes."

There were only so many people she trusted and knew well enough to ask to take care of Alex. Her cousin Jason was one of them, but after Dad had chewed him out over his coverage of the mayoral race, Jason had decided to take a week off to visit his mom in North Carolina. Kendall wouldn't get back from her honeymoon until Friday night, which was still two nights away. The Holcombs were always willing to watch Alex, but it was eleven on a school night and Jenna's ill father lived with them, so Claire wasn't going to call them at this late hour.

She stared at Evan's number on the screen. Would he still be awake? They hadn't seen each other since Sunday. Evan was backlogged with furniture orders he'd put off the week before in order to dedicate time to planning the 5k event, and he'd signed Stella up for doggie obedience classes. All the mayoral challenges, besides the speeches they would give directly before the polls opened, were done. They'd exchanged a few polite texts wishing each other good days, but that had been the extent of their contact.

She pressed the Call button before she lost her nerve.

He didn't answer.

There was no one else. She'd have to pray that her father made it through the night so they could make their peace. So she could try one last time to tell him about God.

Her phone started vibrating. The screen displayed Evan's name. She fumbled to press Accept and was finally successful.

"Sorry I missed your call," Evan explained. "I was taking Stella outside one last time before bed. How are you?"

"Ev… Dad's in the hospital. They say it might be a heart attack. He and I fought yesterday. We haven't made up. What if, what if—"

"Are you home?"

"Yes."

"I'm on my way over." Keys jangled. "Go ahead and keep talking. Stay on with me until I get there, okay?" A door slammed.

She sank down the wall and curled her

knees into her chest. "I'm going to switch you to speaker real quick so I can text my mom."

"Do whatever you need. I'm here." His truck chirped, unlocking. "I'm on my way."

be there soon. leaving house in 10.

"I sent it. I'm back."

The music from his radio filtered over the line for a few seconds until his wireless signal connected and the phone switched to his speakers.

"What happened?"

"Mom said she found him hunched over in the dining room. I don't know much else."

"I meant, you said you fought yesterday."

"I confronted him with everything you told me the other night. About him blackmailing you."

"And?"

"He accused you of lying."

"What did he say I lied about?"

"Well, he admitted to cornering you with the debt and offering to pay it, but he said you turned around and blackmailed him back. That you said you would go marry me and ruin my life unless he paid for Brice's college expenses on top of all the other things he'd promised. He said you had always planned to use me to get something from him."

The only reason that boy pursued you was to get to me. If you can't comprehend that then you know nothing about how this world operates.

"I didn't—"

"I know."

Evan sat in one of the chairs in Claire's apartment playing a game on his phone to pass the time. He probably should have tried to catch a few winks on the couch, but his mind was spinning, and frankly, he was mad.

Sesser had caused so much damage in his life, in the lives of his family members, in Claire's life, and it sounded like he was causing problems for Alex, too. The man continued to destroy and manipulate, and a righteous anger blazed through Evan's chest. If only he could go give Sesser a piece of his mind he'd—

Sesser was dying. If not that, then he was very ill.

Evan's anger leaked away slowly, a pin-prick in a well-worn tire.

It was strange being in the Atwoods' home after all these years. He'd never been allowed beyond the gated entrance, let alone stepped foot inside. Everyone knew the Atwoods were wealthy to the extreme, but he hadn't understood what that meant until now. It made all his successes feel so little and paltry. And that rankled him, too.

Sesser shouldn't have the power to make Evan feel small when the man wasn't even around.

He'd tried not to gawk when Claire met him at the door. They hadn't said much once he arrived. He'd given her a hug and told her to drive safely and take as long as she needed. If she wasn't home in the morning he'd see that Alex got ready for school and onto the bus.

Evan eventually nodded off some time after midnight, but he jolted awake when he heard a door creak. Was Claire home? He blinked and swiveled his head in the direction of the front door. It was closed and there was no sign of her.

"Whoa," Alex said. "You jumped pretty high."

"Buddy." Evan yawned and sat up. He rapidly blinked to clear his contacts so he could focus on the digital screen near the television. Three in the morning. "What are you doing up?"

The kid's black hair stuck out like a wing on one side. "Why are you *here*?"

If Alex had grown up with Sesser as a loving grandfather, Evan would have danced around the question, but from things both Claire and Alex had said, it sounded like Alex didn't have a good relationship with him. Blunt and honest was probably the best way.

"Sesser had an emergency. Your mom and grandma are with him at the hospital right now."

"But not me? It is because I'm not their family." Alex's shoulders slumped. "They say I am, but I'm not."

Evan fought the urge to go over and hug the kid. However, Claire had explained that the psychologist they were seeing thought Alex might have an attachment disorder. If he did, physical contact wasn't always for the best. Evan also knew that if it was true, Alex struggled with feeling alone, unloved and unworthy.

Give me words.

"Hey, you're family. Your mom talks about you all the time." He'd focus on Claire, because he didn't know the dynamics of how Sesser treated Alex. "You're her son, Alex. She loves you so much. That's pretty clear."

The boy dropped down onto the couch.

"They could send me back, if they wanted. They could do it tomorrow."

Evan shook his head hard. He brought his leg up, turning to face Alex on the couch. "That's not going to happen. You don't send back someone you love."

Alex narrowed his eyes. "Mom said you did. I asked her why she looks at you strange and she said because you used to love her but don't anymore."

Evan tightened his gut out of reflex. "When did she say that?"

He shrugged. "Dunno. Maybe after she found out we knew each other. You said you loved her and then sent her back. That's what she told me."

That's how Claire had explained it? Maybe something had been lost in translation.

"Well, listen." Evan relaxed his arm across the back of the couch. "Let's clear some things up here. I love your mom. I want to be with her and never send her back. Understood?"

"But she said—"

"I messed up big-time with her. I'm human, Alex. I sin. I regret it and I've begged her forgiveness for it. God's too."

Alex's chin trembled. He looked away, studied the lines on his palms. "But I like you, and if you can do something like that then my mom could, too."

"Do you love your mom?"

"Yeah, she's cool." He traced his toes back and forth over the shaggy rug in front of the couch and kept his gaze trained on them. "I just… I don't want to…"

"You're afraid of getting attached and losing her."

He worked his toes deeper into the shaggy rug.

Evan finally put his hand on the boy's shoulder. "Are you a Christian, Alex? I mean, I know you come to church with your mom. But do you believe in Jesus?" He tried to find the file in his brain that would help him speak in terms a seven-year-old could understand. Evan had attended training for his roles at the church. "Do you know that once you tell God that you've chosen to be on His team, God will never let you go? It's impossible. He promises that in the Bible."

"You're sure?" Alex's feet stopped moving. He peeked over at Evan.

"I'm positive."

"If you hold a crocodile's mouth shut you give them lockjaw. They're very powerful, but they can't open their mouth or do any damage. I thought of that when you said God doesn't let us go."

Evan considered trying to use the crocodile as an example, but decided against it. Still, he needed to speak on Alex's level. "It's interesting, but I think Mr. Woolly is a better fit here."

"Crocodiles are cooler than caterpillars."

"No doubt." He gave a smile he hoped transmitted warmth and acceptance. "But remember how Mr. Woolly does what he knows he's supposed to do without getting the outcome we all think he should get, but he's faithful, anyway? God doesn't forget Mr. Woolly. When God created animals he set it up so Mr. Woolly would be different, and even after fourteen years, God doesn't forget him or what Mr. Woolly is supposed to become."

"I'm a caterpillar?"

"You're far more important than a caterpillar. If God cares about Mr. Woolly so much and keeps promises to him, just imagine the love He has for you. He loved you so much that He picked Claire to be your mom. He knew you belonged with her. You're exactly where you were always supposed to be. You're home, buddy."

* * *

Evan's boots thumped along the shined floors of the heart wing of the hospital. If he paused outside Sesser's door he risked losing his gumption, so he strode right in.

"Get. Out. You're not welcome here." Sesser's scowl almost made Evan turn tail and run.

Almost.

"I know." Evan came a few feet into the room. That was far enough.

"My wife was in here earlier. Singing your praises." He spat and dragged the back of his hand over his mouth. His fingers trembled. "I never thought I'd hear that fool woman ever speak of your kind like that."

Claire's mom had hugged Evan after they'd returned, and thanked him for watching Alex. He and Claire had speechlessly watched her head up the stairs after that. The kindness from Mrs. Atwood had bolstered Evan's idea to try to make peace with Sesser. If her parents could accept him, it would make life easier for Claire in the long run.

"Sir, I know you don't like me."

"You've got that right."

"And you never wanted to have to deal with me again."

"I don't and I won't." Sesser tapped his IV.

"If they didn't have me tied to this bed with tubes I'd bull rush you out of here myself. Don't think I couldn't."

"The problem is I love your daughter." Evan widened his stance. "And I'm not going anywhere, not when it comes to Claire."

"I will have you arrested!" Sesser's voice rose. "I'll come after your house. I'll start by kicking you out of your business."

"On what grounds?" Sesser owned the building Evan rented in town for Goose Harbor Furniture, but he could find another. He would. Claire was worth a setback in his business. "I love her and if she wants me, I'll spend the rest of my life being there for her. I wish you could see that all I want is what's best for Claire."

Sesser shook his head, his jowls jiggling like a bulldog's. His cheeks and a wide patch of hairless scalp at the top of his head flashed red. "I *know* what's best for my daughter, and it's not you!"

"I'm sorry you feel that way but—"

"I dated your ma. Didn't know that, did you?" Sesser shoved his hands against the bed rails to hike himself up higher. "Mason was chasing her, too, and she ended up choosing him. Look at how well that worked out for her. Sheryl had a good life waiting and she tossed it away on a worthless no-good. He professed love, too. She hates him now, doesn't she? Wishes she had stuck with me. Think how different her life would be."

Evan tried not to show how Sesser's words affected him, but his insides felt as if someone had shoved them into a slingshot and let them fly. His mom had dated *Sesser*? No wonder she had so much anger toward Brice. She'd made no secret of the fact that she was stuck with their dad because she'd gotten pregnant with Brice. She must have watched Sesser's life from afar and known that it could have been hers all along.

Sesser's grin turned wicked. He knew he was getting to Evan.

How would life be different if his mom had married Sesser?

"Claire wouldn't exist."

Sesser waved his hand in the air. "I wouldn't know to miss her."

Evan curled his fingers into fists. The man was impossible. How could he regard his only child so flippantly? "All I wanted was for us to come to a civil understanding. I just want peace."

"You'll get peace from me when I'm dead." Sesser thumped his chest and then winced. "How's that for understanding?"

Evan's phone rang. He fished it out of his pocket and saw Claire was calling. "I have to take this."

"If you go after her, you're no different than your pa, hear me?"

Enough. Evan strode out of the room and walked down the hall. He was done listening to the man's poison.

"Evan?" Claire's voice sounded off. Tears?

He put some distance between himself and Sesser's room before finding a wall to lean against. "Everything okay?"

"Alex told me you talked to him about God last night. Ev, he just asked me to pray with him. Alex just became a Christian."

"That's wonderful!" Evan was a grown man, but he wanted to jump up and down. If he'd been home or at work, instead of in the middle of a hospital, he would have. "I can't wait to see him."

"Thank you. You…you reach him in a way that I can't."

"Not true." He made his way down the hallway to the elevators. "There's a reason he came to you for the most important part. He loves you, Claire. He just has a hard time knowing what to do with it."

There was a long pause.

"Tomorrow's our speeches."

"Big day." The bell rang above the elevator.

"I was thinking…only if you wanted to, of course…" Was she nervous? "We could meet beforehand and go in side by side. Take the stage together and present a united front. Kind of, no matter who you choose to vote for on Monday, we'll both work toward improving Goose Harbor. Do you think that's silly?"

"I think it's brilliant."

"Meet me at the swing set then? Where Jason took our pictures."

"I'll be there. But Claire?"

"What is it?"

"I'm looking forward to *after* the election far more than the speeches tomorrow night." When they could talk about the possibility of *them*.

Chapter Fourteen

"The election is only a few days away now." Kendall slid into the other side of the booth. Her skin was tan from a week spent on a beach in Cancún for her honeymoon. She and Brice had returned late last night.

"I'll be happy when it's all over." Claire took a swig of her peanut butter chocolate malt. They'd picked to meet at Cherry Top Café for lunch instead of their usual Saturday morning coffee date. Kendall's plane had been delayed and she'd wanted to sleep in. Being the weekend, the café was packed.

The restaurant smelled of grease and fried cheese, and something about that mixture was oddly comforting.

Kendall eyed her. "Are you prepared for either outcome?"

Claire bobbed her head. "I honestly don't

care which one of us wins come Monday. Evan loves Goose Harbor. If he becomes the mayor he'll do everything he can to keep this place wonderful. And if I win, that's great, too."

"This is a one-eighty from the last time we talked." She stole one of Claire's fries and twirled it in a circle. "Not that I'm complaining. Warm and fuzzy suits you, but what gives?"

Kendall was Claire's only close girlfriend and she'd been bursting to tell someone the truth. How she felt about Evan was not a topic of conversation her mother would welcome, and she definitely wasn't going to call Jason to discuss it. That left only Kendall.

"I love him. I don't know what else to say. But that changes everything. I love Evan."

"Claire!" Kendall snatched her hand and squeezed hard enough to feel like she might dislocate something. "I prayed for this! Evan told me about your guys' past, but I felt like there was *more* for you two. I told him to be careful with your heart, but I do believe his intentions are good."

Kendall had been praying for them? Claire's heart swelled.

"We decided to wait until after the election, but… I can't imagine a future without him next to me." She'd had a difficult enough time convincing herself not to invent a reason to show up at his business or on his doorstep every day during the last week. Evan had worked his way into her life, her thoughts, her heart so completely. "Do you know what I mean?"

"Hello!" Kendall wiggled her ring finger. "Gonna have to say I understand completely." She folded her hands on the table. "I'm so happy. Look at this stupid grin." She pointed at her wide, goofy smile. "I'm so proud of you. After Brice explained, I wasn't sure how you'd react when you found out about their plans."

Claire dragged her last fry through the ketchup. "Whose plans?"

Kendall blew her bangs out of her eyes. "You know, how if Evan becomes mayor he's going to work it so Brice can build another dock in town. That's the entire reason he's running. Didn't he tell you about it?"

"He didn't."

"Oh." Kendall's grin disappeared. "He didn't?"

Claire fought against the frustration bubbling inside her. Kendall had kept that from her?

She pushed her plate to the center of the table. "Why didn't you?"

"Brice told me while we were on vacation." Kendall wove a napkin through her fingers. She started to tear off little shreds. "I had no clue before then. Promise. I'd been busy with wedding plans."

Claire believed Kendall and her heart went out to her friend. Kendall was forced to walk a tightrope between the man she loved and the woman she'd become best friends with. Now that Kendall was married, Brice would always come first. That's how it should be.

Claire ran her fingers through her hair and began to tug, and then froze. That mannerism belonged to Evan and she wanted no part of it. "That will hurt my father's business in town."

If Brice built a dock and offered cheaper rates, everyone would pull off of both of the Atwood docks. Brice could undercut them significantly to woo clients. A significant part of her father's income came from fees collected on products being shipped in and out of Goose Harbor through the docks.

"Well, it's a monopoly right now." Kendall tore into a second napkin. "Do you think that's the best for everyone?"

"I work for my father's company at the moment, so it's my job to care about him losing revenue." Dad losing money wasn't what bothered her, though. It wasn't what made it feel as if someone had stuck screws into her chest and turned them. If Evan had been honest and told her the plan, if he'd trusted her... But it had all been a lie, hadn't it?

"I can't believe this. Evan..." She gasped. "That's what this was all about. My dad was right. All along."

A vent overhead kicked on and started to spew hot air. Being inside was stifling. Tightness clawed up Claire's sides. The homey grease smell now made her gag. She needed fresh air. Needed to be alone.

Claire tossed cash onto the table and gathered her belongings. "I have to go."

Kendall caught her arm. "For what it's worth, I'm sorry."

Claire nodded once and then turned and rushed out of the café.

How many times had Dad told her that *all* people would view her in relation to what they could get from him? It would always be about her dad. Evan's sweet words, all the romantic moments and reliving of the past they'd done had been for him to—once again—get something for his brother. He'd used Claire, and worse, he'd used Alex.

Perhaps her father hadn't been lying about him reversing the blackmail, either.

She checked her watch. Two hours until the meeting at town hall.

Two hours until she exposed a rat.

Evan dragged his shoes through the snow, slowing the swing. He'd been outside waiting for thirty minutes in a coat that wasn't quite warm enough for lengthy exposure.

Claire would show. Of course she would show.

What if she didn't?

Is this how she'd felt on the courthouse steps?

He stomped his feet to warm up. Checked his phone again. No new messages. Today she hadn't responded to any of his texts, which was odd, especially for a Saturday. Then again, her father was still in the hospital and she was probably there with him. Or Alex had a Scouts meeting. There were a number of reasons.

Ten minutes ago, Evan had watched people stream into the town hall. He pictured Mr. Banks pacing the stage, looking for them.

Where are you?

He waited five more minutes. Two more after that. Looked at his phone again.

Worry roared in his chest and pounded in his ears. What if something had happened to her? Maybe someone inside town hall knew what was going on. He jogged down the path, across the square and into the building.

Claire's voice filled the meeting room. "My opponent doesn't care about this town. Not like he's led you to believe."

Concerned murmurs bounced around the room. People shook their heads and turned to whisper with their neighbors.

Her gaze scanned the room, landing on certain people, making eye contact. "Once he takes office, his plans are to use his political position to grant special favors and permits to members of his family. That has been his aim all along. He plans to destroy long-standing businesses so he can give money to the people he deems worthy."

Oh, no. The dock.

Sickness rolled like a lopsided soccer ball through his gut. He should have come clean to her about Brice pushing him to run and why. But it hadn't come up and once they started spending time together, it had been the furthest thing from his mind.

She finally spotted him in the back of the room. Her eyes bored into his. "Evan Daniels knows nothing beyond using and manipulating people. He pretends to care, only as long as it benefits him."

Evan's knees wobbled. He grabbed on to a nearby chair for support. He finally found his voice. "Let me explain. Please, Claire." Every head whipped in his direction. As if he was facing a pack of circling wolves, he held up his hands.

Mr. Banks loudly cleared his throat. "Please refrain from delaying us with any more outbursts. You'll have your turn, Mr. Daniels. When Miss Atwood is done with the floor."

Overhead lights made the moisture in her eyes gleam. "With the tourist season dawning, we can't afford to trust our future to someone who only looks out for himself. Who believes love is a commodity. Goose Harbor is better than that. Vote with a conscience."

A smattering of applause followed her retreat from the podium. She backed toward the edge of the stage, where Evan knew there was a door to a narrow staircase. The din of confused and curious neighbors talking to each other made it impossible to think.

Evan zigzagged around people standing in the aisle. He hopped over a chair and made it to the back staircase just in time to hook Claire's arm. "Why didn't you come to me with that?"

Spinning on her heels, she shoved his hand off her arm. "Why didn't *you* tell *me*? No, don't bother answering that. I don't care. Not about this election. Not about what people think of me. And certainly not about whatever sob story full of excuses you want to share."

He jammed his hands into his hair. Rocked on his feet. "I know it looks bad."

Her glare could have melted granite. "All the attention, the late night talks, the kiss and your time spent with Alex—all lies, all an act, so Brice could have a stupid little dock."

"None of that was an act. I love you. Please, Claire. I love you."

"You actually think I'd believe you?" Her laugh held no humor. "How's the saying go? Fool me once, shame on you. Fool me twice... At least there's no fear of that. Did you actually think I was dumb enough to fall for you again? Well, I'm not." She gripped the railing and turned away from him.

The door behind Evan whooshed open.

Mr. Banks sopped at his forehead with a grimy handkerchief. "It's high time you took the stage, Mr. Daniels. People are liable to riot if you don't do something to calm them!"

Evan kept his gaze glued to Claire's back, willing her to turn around, to hear him out.

"Go." Her voice was pure ice.

"Claire."

"I'm busy, Mr. Daniels. I have to go explain to a seven-year-old boy that the man he believes to be a hero is a liar who can't be trusted. I have to go tell him that another person in his life wasn't worth getting attached to. I have to—" A sob broke off her words. Claire rushed down the steps.

Banks seized Evan's arm before he could follow. "There is a roomful of townspeople in there."

The back door slammed. Claire was gone.

Evan bowed his head and finally nodded, following Banks back into the meeting room. He held his hands up to quiet the crowd. "Claire was right. I only sought the position at my brother's urging and we do dream of building another dock in town and thought me being mayor couldn't hurt our chances at getting approval granted. However, as of this moment I am stepping out of the mayoral race. Claire remains blameless in all of this. She is a strong and determined leader who could do our community proud. Vote for her."

Chapter Fifteen

❧

Someone jiggled his doorknob. They were using a key to enter, since he hadn't answered their knocks. Evan stared at the half-eaten container of ice cream melting on his counter, not even caring about the mess it would make. Stella pawed at the back door, wanting to be let out one more time before bed.

Brice and Kendall exchanged sad looks as they entered his house.

"We heard about the meeting. People were talking about it at church today. You okay?" Kendall didn't bother taking off her coat or boots. She joined him in the kitchen and wrapped him in a hug. "I'm sorry. I think this is my fault."

Evan patted her back. "You told the truth. You have nothing to feel sorry for. I'm the only one in this situation who did something wrong."

Kendall didn't let go. "She'll come around."

Evan eased out of her hold. "Does it matter? I went and saw Sesser in the hospital. I tried to make peace and he said I could only have that over his dead body. It's better this way. She's better off without me."

A muscle in Brice's jaw popped. "Other way around—you're better off without her."

Protectiveness over Claire roared to life in Evan's chest. Brice might be his brother and his best friend, but Evan wouldn't let him speak badly about the woman he loved. "I know you don't like Sesser, but what have you got against Claire?"

Brice's eyebrows shot up. "She's toyed with you for half your life."

"Toyed with me? How about flip that around." He drew a circle in the air with his finger. "I'm the one who left her at the courthouse, and she wasn't wrong to share what she did at the meeting. Those *were* our plans and I deliberately didn't tell her about them."

"She made it sound like we were trying to hurt the town. As if we were Sesser Atwood, ruled by greed. We want that dock to help the community. Our intention wasn't to line our pockets, but that's how she painted it."

"Intentions don't always matter." His talk with Claire about flirting came to mind. "You can have the best intentions and still end up hurting someone."

"But the dock was important. It was—"

"I don't care about the dock!" Evan tossed his hands in the air and stalked to the other side of the kitchen. "Can't you see that? My life is falling apart and all you can talk about is that stupid dock."

"You used to care about it, too."

"See, that's where you're wrong. I never cared about it. I never wanted to be mayor. I did it because that's what you wanted, and for so many years I've made my choices based on what's best for you. How I can make you proud. I can't do that anymore." Evan shoved his hands against his counter, savoring the coolness, and hung his head. "I can't—I've lost everything."

"What are you talking about?"

"She told me to tell you. Said you deserved to know." Evan launched into the details of Sesser's blackmailing. Every part of it. Brice stumbled into a seat. He listened with his head in his hands and then stayed that way a long time after Evan's story was done. Kendall squeezed Evan's shoulder before taking the seat next to Brice and picking up his hand.

Brice's head lifted and the green eyes that mirrored Evan's own sought him out. A breath rattled through his older brother. "He paid my tuition? He's the reason I have a degree? I can't comment on that... I'll need time to process. But I need you to understand that you don't owe me anything. You never did."

Their dad had beat Brice senseless more times than Evan wanted to remember. Evan had crouched out of sight until Dad's anger burned off. He'd never pulled him off of Brice. Brice was selfless; he deserved a happy life with Kendall. Evan? Most days he still felt less than a man for allowing it all to happen.

Evan's vision blurred. "When I goaded Dad, when I thought I was too funny for my own good...every time he lunged at me, every single time he came at me with his fists up, you were there. You stepped in front. Blocked me. I let you take those hits. Hits meant for me. Again and again, and I never once—"

"And it was my choice to step in front of his fists and take the blows with your name on them." Brice met his gaze. "My choice, Evan. No one made me do it and I didn't do it to get something from you."

"But I could have tried to stop him. Half the time it was my fault that he was mad." Evan pinched the bridge of his nose and tried to block out the memories of their father's wrath. "I keep trying to do something to make it up to you, but it never feels like enough for everything you suffered. So yes, now that we're older, if you want something, I'll do anything to get it for you. That's why I ran for mayor."

Brice let go of Kendall's hand, rested his elbows on his knees and rubbed his palms together. "You are no longer a victim, so stop putting yourself in that box. None of us are victims any longer."

Where had that come from? "I don't pretend to be a victim."

"You tried to pay back what you viewed as a sacrifice by sacrificing your relationship with Claire *twice* now." Brice spoke slowly, carefully, as if he was explaining a difficult concept to a child. "I'm going to say this once, so listen up. Don't cheapen my sacrifice by feeling guilty when it was my choice. You are not allowed to carry that burden on your shoulders any longer. You were worth it. Each kick and hit and verbal assault. You were worth it every single time."

"But why?" Evan's voice broke and he didn't try to hide it. "I don't understand. I've never been able to understand."

"I love you. It's as simple and complicated as that."

Kendall set her hand on Brice's knee. "God loves you like that, too, Evan. You realize that, don't you?"

"I'm a Christian."

"That's not what I asked. A person can be a Christian and still struggle with feeling less-than, worthless and undeserving. God doesn't want you to feel that way. The cross was the moment when God whispered, 'I love you and you are worth this much to Me.' We risk cheapening God's sacrifice when we deem ourselves undeserving. I know I've been guilty of doing that sometimes."

"I think I've been doing that my whole life. What am I going to do, guys? I'm a complete mess."

Brice rose and made his way to his brother. "Welcome to the club."

Residents filled the meeting room to bursting on Monday night. Voting had occurred during the town hall's business hours and had been tabulated before the special board meeting. Some of the local shop owners had closed early in order to secure seats in the front. Claire kept her gaze trained on the floor while they visited around her. Excitement pulsed in the air, as if they were at a prizefight instead of a perfunctory assembly.

Mrs. Clarkson squeezed down the crowded aisle to claim the empty seat beside Claire.

Claire clasped Alex's hand. After Mr. Banks announced that she was their new mayor, she'd keep her speech short. She'd apologize for her outburst on Saturday, thank them for their votes and promise to lead them with a more level head than she'd recently displayed.

Mr. Banks tapped the microphone. "No one is happier than I am that this election is over. Our new mayor will take office next Monday, which means I'll be stepping down at the end of this week. I'd love to be able to say that I've enjoyed my time serving in the interim position, but I haven't, and you are all aware of that already, so let's move on."

He began to open an envelope. His hand trembled with age. The page inside crinkled as he drew it out. He read the sheet, once, twice, a third time before clearing his throat. "It seems the person who won did so by the wildly unorthodox method of being a write-in candidate."

Whispers carried around the room, but Claire couldn't hear them. A write-in candidate? She'd lost. They didn't want her, even when she was the only choice.

Mr. Banks lofted the page into the air.

"The next mayor of Goose Harbor is Kellen Ashby!"

Kellen's daughters sprang to their feet, screaming and jumping up and down. Skylar ran to the stage, snatched the page from Mr. Banks and performed a victory dance that rivaled any on the football field. Kellen's face had gone red. The poor man looked petrified.

Claire's initial shock faded and she couldn't help but chuckle. If she had to lose to someone, Kellen wasn't so bad. He was a great guy who would serve the community well.

Mrs. Clarkson slipped her arm around Claire. "Try not to feel bad, dear. This town always did run better with an Ashby at the helm."

Claire got to her feet and addressed the crowd. "You all chose well. Kellen will make a great mayor." She sent a smile his way to show him she was sincerely happy for him and wanted him to accept the position. "Much better than I would have been."

The crowd responded by converging in Kellen's direction, and Claire took that as her cue to sneak away. She kept hold of Alex's hand and led him out the back way, down the narrow stairwell where she'd fought with Evan. Now that she'd had two days to cool off, she regretted how she'd handled the blowup with him. She'd allowed emotions to rule her and didn't want to make that mistake again.

When the time came she'd apologize to him, if he would hear her out. She'd told her father about Brice and Evan's plans to build the dock and her father's irate response had embarrassed her. He was her parent, but he was spiteful, mean-hearted and greedy. Kendall had explained how breaking Dad's monopoly would be a positive step for the community, and after considering it, Claire couldn't help but agree.

Late Saturday, guilt had shrouded her shoulders like a heavy woolen quilt. She'd spent her entire life being supported by the money her father had pinched out of the people of Goose Harbor and other nearby communities. She knew most of his business practices were dishonorable and she'd turned a blind eye. Evan's point about messes being hidden under the snow came to mind. He'd been right. Stepping out on her own was scary, but she could no longer ignore the evil her father engaged in.

Claire had immediately typed up and handed in her resignation from the family company. She'd also informed her parents that she and Alex would be moving out as soon as they could. Now came the task of finding a new home.

She and Alex walked toward her car, winter air tickling her face. "Well, buddy, where do you think we should go to celebrate?"

"There's nothing to celebrate. You lost." He gave her a skeptical look, as if she might be trying to trick him.

"There's plenty to celebrate." She looped her arm over his spindly shoulders. "Besides, you're the man in my life and I want to go do something. What should we do?"

"I'm a boy." Alex stopped abruptly. "Evan's the man in your life."

"Evan and I...we decided not to be friends anymore." That sounded a lot better than admitting to her son that she'd all but thrown a public hissy fit because she believed Evan didn't love her.

Alex narrowed his eyes. "I don't think that's truth."

"Well, it—"

"He told me he loves you." Alex pushed his fingertips into his chest. "He loves you with the kind of love that never sends someone back."

Claire dropped to her knees to be at his

eye level. Snow seeped through her pant legs. "Sweetheart."

"He said he'd never send you back, Mom." Alex's voice grew stronger. "That means no matter what you do or what happens you're his family. No send-backs. Like me and you. It's love forever that doesn't go away."

How could she make Alex understand that no matter how much she wanted to change things, Evan might not end up in their life?

"Listen to the kid. He talks a lot of sense." Evan's voice put her off balance and she had to catch herself with her hands to the ground.

Alex helped steady her. Claire rose to her feet and a stiff wind whipped her hair in front of her face. She pawed at the strands until she could finally see the man she loved leaning against the hood of her car. "Evan?"

He was here. She tried not to read too much into it. Evan wasn't one to let a feud fester—well, besides with her father. But that was different. He could have sought her out to make peace, not to reopen their tattered love story.

He straightened as she and Alex drew nearer. "I'm sorry I didn't tell you about the dock. The truth is, I never wanted to be mayor."

"She lost, too." Alex jutted his thumb in her direction.

"Kellen won by a write-in vote," Claire explained.

Evan broke into a dimpled grin. "If that isn't the most Goose Harbor thing ever."

She nodded, inching closer. "I thought it was a fitting end."

His dimples disappeared. He shuffled his feet and then stopped to search her face with his intense green eyes. "Can you ever forgive me?" he whispered.

Claire stretched her hand out, offering it, waiting for him to take it. He did.

She closed her fingers around his, thankful she'd forgotten her gloves despite the cold. She traced the calluses on his work-worn hands. "I realized when I was praying yesterday that if you had wanted to use me, you wouldn't have stepped down. I overreacted and I'm sorry for everything I said. What must everyone think?"

Evan captured her other hand so they were facing each other. He swung their hands between them. "All I care about right now is *your* opinion of me." He stopped fidgeting with her hands and captured her gaze with his. He drank in the sight of her cheeks, her lips, her eyes. "Claire, after everything, do I have any chance of winning you back?"

Taking him by surprise, she rose up on her tiptoes and kissed him gently before pulling back. "You can't win back something you've never lost." She looped her hands around his neck. "I have loved you since I was a teenager and I want to love you until my age hits triple digits. No one challenges me the way you do. No one uplifts me or enrages me quite like you, either."

"What about your dad? I don't want to come between you and your family."

"That's my choice to make. Alex here…" She reached out and draped an arm over her son's shoulder, bringing him into their huddle. "He's taught me something really important. God makes families, not by bloodlines but by heart ties." She tapped Evan's chest twice. "My heart is tied to yours, Evan Daniels. I want *you* to be my family."

"And me." Alex scooted so he was between them. "I have heart ties to both of you, too."

"Speaking of my dad, it just so happens that I gave him my two-weeks notice." She added in a softer voice, "I don't want to be under his thumb ever again."

Alex propped his foot on the bumper of her car. "We're moving out, too. We started packing yesterday. But we don't know where we're going. Right, Mom?"

Evan rocked back on the balls of his feet and a playful smirk lit his face. "Well, that's funny, because I have plenty of space in my house."

Claire tilted her head and grinned at him. "Is that so?"

"But I'm not looking for roommates, you understand." Evan closed the distance between them again. "These spots in my house, they're only available for family of the heart-tied variety. You wouldn't happen to know any people who fit that description, would you?"

"Us!" Alex jumped back into the conversation. "We do!"

"Under one condition." Claire held up a finger.

"I'm listening." Evan fought a goofy grin. Unsuccessfully.

Claire stood there taking him in for a second. She loved him, every facet of his personality, and she wanted to be with him forever. They'd waited long enough. "We go to the courthouse tomorrow and do what we planned to do twelve years ago. We rewrite our ending."

Evan drew her into his arms. He kissed her

forehead and moved down to her cheek, her nose, her other cheek. "We'll go." He pressed his lips to hers. "But we don't rewrite anything," he whispered, his breath hot against her neck. "Instead, we'll write a new beginning. All of us."

* * * * *

Don't miss these other
GOOSE HARBOR *stories*
from Jessica Keller:

THE WIDOWER'S SECOND CHANCE
THE FIREMAN'S SECRET
THE SINGLE DAD NEXT DOOR
SMALL-TOWN GIRL
APPLE ORCHARD BRIDE

Available now from Love Inspired!

Find more great reads at
www.LoveInspired.com

Dear Reader,

Have you ever felt weighted down by expectations? Perhaps like Claire, you have family members who pressure you to reach a certain level of success. Or maybe like Evan, you set impossible expectations for yourself.

Expectations and goals aren't bad, but when our lives become ruled by what we accomplish or strive for, when we tie our self-worth to whether or not we meet a certain goal, that's a problem.

While Evan made a lot of life choices in order to please his brother, he was also striving to earn God's approval. In the end, Evan was the one who told Alex, "Do you know that once you tell God that you've chosen to be on His team, God will never let you go?"

God will never let you go. No matter what. Hear that. Take it in. Believe it.

Thank you for spending time with Evan and Claire. I hope you enjoyed their story. I love interacting with readers, so make sure to look me up on social media or at www.jessicakellerbooks.com and say hi!

Dream big,
Jess